USA TODAY BESTSELLING AUTHOR

Dale Mayer

MAN DOWN

JASPER

JASPER: MAN DOWN, BOOK 1
Beverly Dale Mayer
Valley Publishing Ltd.

ISBN-13: 978-1-778863-18-9
Print Edition

Books in This Series:

Jasper, Book 1

Masters, Book 2

About This Book

There is no greater motive than bloodlust, DNA, and revenge mixed up in a cocktail of hatred …

Jasper, watching Mason go down, is all-in on the investigation. Taking over the current investigation team, he distrusts everyone. Tesla, his cousin, expects Jasper to get to the bottom of this and fast.

ER nurse Amber isn't on Mason's team but knows something major is happening. The hospital is overwhelmed with men, as they want updates on Mason's condition. A few look like they belong, and then a couple don't. Taking pictures of those in question, she sends them to Jasper, which starts a cascading chain of events. And none of it good.

Hunting down Mason's shooter, Jasper is sidelined by keeping Amber safe, when she's targeted next. He must keep them both safe, … even as the investigation heats up and gets even uglier.

Sign up to be notified of all Dale's releases here!
https://geni.us/DaleNews

PROLOGUE

THE PLANE TOUCHED down in a controlled smooth movement, hardly jarring the few passengers seated inside. A gorgeous blue sky was outside, a typical sunny California day.

Mason and several other men from the Shadow Recon team waited for the plane to come to a full stop. When it finally stopped rolling, Mason grabbed his bags, tired, happy, but somewhat sad.

As answers went, the ones the team had found in the Arctic training base hadn't been the easiest. At the core was fear and self-preservation. Such common human failings and, in this one case, one with massive consequences, as individually the men involved had slid deeper and deeper into their lies and deceit.

The fact that Elijah had reached out and had contacted Mason directly would help his case but not enough, though it sounded as if the cancer would likely take him pretty damn quickly anyway. Still, he wanted to answer as many questions about as many cases as he could, so some families could find some closure.

Mason wanted that too. Families were still suffering, as they looked for answers to the deaths of their loved ones.

Deaths that were meaningless, senseless, and all the more painful for the betrayal by these men, who should have supported their military brethren, not taking them down, not making them victims.

When the back door to the plane opened, and Mason walked out onto the tarmac, he held up a hand to shield his eyes, wishing he'd brought his sunglasses with him because it was a bright sunny day. Tesla was planning to pick him up, and they would spend a few days together, before he headed back to the office, his field mission over.

He headed for the main hangar, falling in behind the other men. He had places to go to, but chances were good that Tesla would be here somewhere, waiting. And she never did what he expected of her. She was her own person, a special soul, and he was blessed every day to come home to her.

Hearing a shout off to the side, he turned and caught sight of her, hopping out of the Jeep and rushing toward him, her pregnant belly bouncing lightly with every step.

Mason grinned and laughed, as she opened her arms and raced toward him. He dropped his bag and raced in her direction.

He hadn't made it ten steps when an odd *ping* hit his head, and he was stopped in his tracks, a slow paralysis taking over his body. He stared at his beloved wife, watching her confusion, then her horror, followed then by her scream that seemed ripped from her very soul.

Mason's knees buckled, even as he recognized the red flow covering him was his blood. He collapsed to the asphalt beneath him, and the world around him went black and silent, … as he was sucked into the murky darkness.

CHAPTER 1

J ASPER RACED TOWARD the crowd as people called out in a frenzy, "Man down! Man down!" Up ahead, desperately trying to get to her husband, Tesla struggled to get through the masses. With her rounded belly, she was in danger of getting knocked over or injured in some other way. Jasper quickly came up behind her, and, wrapping his arms around her, swung her off to the side and whispered in a hushed voice, "I'll get to him and determine his status. You stay here."

She half buckled against him, as he gently put her on her feet, out of the way of the chaos all around them. Then he turned and quickly fought his way to Mason's side.

Mason, his eyes open, stared skyward, but it was obvious that he was in shock. Blood poured from the gunshot wound to his head, and Jasper caught a glimpse of shattered bone behind it. It seemed as if the bullet must have hit the bone, pushing the fragment outward, and then traveling through to the ground somewhere behind Mason. "Somebody find that damn bullet," Jasper barked, and others scattered.

Frowning, Jasper dropped down beside another man, who was working on Mason. "Are the EMTs on the way?"

The man, with his hand and a piece of cloth on Mason's

head wound, gave a curt nod. "They are. We need to get him stabilized …" He let his voice trail off.

Jasper immediately checked over the rest of Mason. A bullet wound appeared on his lower abdomen. Jasper immediately ripped off part of his shirt, folded it quickly, and applied pressure to stop the bleeding from that wound too.

The other guy nodded at him in approval. "Nobody saw anything, of course," he said in a clipped tone, as he turned to look at the crowd that still remained.

Immediately everybody nearby shook their heads.

"From this angle, I would call it as a sniper atop that roof," Jasper said, pointing to the red building off to the side. "Get a team over there now."

With that, several men took off. He hoped that others had heard the shots and were already pursuing the gunman, so that the guys heading there now were just secondary assistance. Now, Jasper heard the sirens of emergency vehicles racing toward them. He looked over at the other guy, realized it was Masters, and asked in a low voice, "Chances?"

"It's Mason," Masters said curtly. "In other cases, not much chance, but it's him," he added, shaking his head. "And he's got everything in the world to live for," he murmured, as he cast a glance to where Tesla stood, still vertical, but barely, as she stared out at the crowd, her face white, shock and fear evident in her gaze. "I've got this, if you want to deal with her," Masters offered.

"I'll deal with her once we get Mason squared away with the EMTs," Jasper murmured.

"You are family, aren't you?"

He gave him a small smile. "Yeah, cousins by marriage."

"That's family, and she'll need it."

"She'll also need answers," he said, his voice determined.

Masters frowned at him. "You're not active military though, are you?"

"I am, although not exactly with a popular division."

"Oh, shit, are you upstairs?"

"Somewhat, yeah. Let's just say, *an unpopular department.*" He chuckled. "Still, that could be exactly what we need right now."

Masters didn't say anything for a long moment, then he nodded. "Let's hope not."

"The sniper must have balls of stone on him." Trying to fight back the fear overtaking his thoughts as he stared down at Mason, Jasper murmured, "And I'm sure he's long gone now."

"Do you know something we don't?"

"Not yet"—Jasper glared around—"but you can bet I'll be hunting this one down myself."

"I'm sure you will," Masters agreed, checking Mason's pulse yet again. "If you need a hand, you let me know."

"I'll need a hand, guaranteed," he said, looking over at him.

"This won't be a one-person job." Masters shifted his hand pressure on Mason's head wound, looking around to see if help was near. Lowering his voice, he asked, "Any idea what's going on?"

"Not yet, but this was too well-thought-out. Somebody knew when he was flying in, what shape he would be in, and where he was going next, so …"

Masters sucked in his breath. "Are you seriously suggesting an inside job?"

"I'm not saying anything," Jasper replied, his tone hardening as the paramedics arrived, quickly moving the two of them back, so they could take over Mason's care. "I'll take Tesla to the hospital." Jasper noted her hovering close to the paramedics.

"You better clean up first."

"Tesla is tougher than that," he said, with a shrug. "She won't give a shit about my being covered in blood. She'll just want to be with Mason," he said, turning toward her. "I'll clean up at the hospital." And, with that, he raced to Tesla, who was now sitting on the ground, rocking, her arms wrapped around her belly, as she watched her husband get loaded onto a gurney. As Jasper approached, she took one look at him and winced.

He nodded. "Yes, it's Mason's blood, and it's serious. He's been shot twice. We don't know if there are more injuries. Let's get you and Mason to the hospital."

He reached out a bloody hand that he'd done his best to wipe on his jeans, but no way to soften the full effect of the fact that he was covered in her husband's blood. He knew more than most how Mason and Tesla had forged a close, tight-knit union and what it would do to her should Mason be lost.

Still, she reached up and grasped Jasper's hand firmly. "Just get me there," she grunted, her tone harsh.

"I'm planning on it," he said. "Let's go."

AS SOON AS Jasper settled Tesla into the passenger seat, he walked to the back of his vehicle. He pulled out a clean shirt and stripped off the bloody one he now wore. Using other medical supplies he kept on hand, he did his best to wipe off as much blood as he could, tossing it all back in the trunk. Then he got in the driver's seat and pulled out.

"What do you know about Masters?" he asked Tesla in a clipped tone.

With a sigh, she stated, "I don't know anything about him. He's just around."

"Was he supposed to pick up Mason?"

She thought about it but obviously was struggling to concentrate.

"Stay focused. We must collect as much information as we can, and fast. So I need you to tell me everything you can think of."

She took a deep breath and nodded. "I hear you. … I do. … I'm just not sure I have an answer."

"Better than making one up," he replied, with a smile.

"Not something I would ever do," she murmured.

"You know as well as I do that we've got to get to the bottom of this—and fast."

"He was targeted, wasn't he?" She spoke in a whisper.

"Absolutely. He got off that plane with no opportunity to do anything but take a full hit," Jasper confirmed. "So the question is, who set this up?"

She shook her head, her bottom lip trembling a bit. "Everybody loves Mason."

Jasper wouldn't argue with her because obviously somebody did *not* love Mason, but Jasper knew what she meant. Generally Mason was highly respected by both those below and above him, but there would always be somebody crosswise for some reason. An outlier would work to make life miserable for him. And that was just the current way of the world. Whenever you had somebody who succeeded, somebody else chose to work against that success. Obviously somebody was determined to interrupt or to derail Mason's intentions.

Jasper glanced at Tesla. "Stay strong." Her back stiffened, as he smirked in response. "There's my girl."

She snorted. "Always the same Jasper. You might not know me as well as you think."

"I never claimed to. All I need to know right now is that you'll make it through this," he explained, "and that you'll do your darndest to not let Mason know how upset you are and how worried you are about his making it through this."

She continued to glare at him. "Mason knows that I'll be there for whatever needs to be done, no matter the outcome."

"Good. So I'll be straight with you. I didn't see anything close to his spine, so I highly doubt we'll hear of any paralysis or the like. I'm more concerned about his surviving. I won't minimize the damage. I saw a lot of bleeding." She swallowed and nodded. "Yet he'll get the very best medical attention available, and you can bet they are already on it."

"Right." She took a deep breath.

He listened cautiously, hoping that she wouldn't hyperventilate on him. Sure enough, she pulled herself back into a state of calm control. He gave her a small smile. "You're doing great. Let's keep it that way."

She didn't say anything to that and took a moment to take stock. "You will find out who did this, won't you?"

"I plan to. There'll be one hell of an investigation."

"Good." She turned to him, declaring, "You also know this was an inside job."

He winced. "I was hoping you wouldn't pick up on that quite so fast."

"Like hell I wouldn't. Shot on base, by sniper fire, with

enough skill to take that shot and to not miss," she summed up. "So, even if it wasn't somebody who is currently on base, maybe somebody just not currently on active duty, … you must know perfectly well that somebody coming from that background had an intel contact inside."

"Potentially," he admitted, "but let's not rule out the fact that we could be dealing with a foreign entity as well."

She sat back, pondering it silently.

"You and I both know that, as Mason has climbed the ranks, he's also made enemies." She stiffened, but he shook his head. "No, this isn't a time to sugarcoat it. Enemies, they happen to all of us. That doesn't mean that Mason's any less of a man, any less of that perfect person you love so well," he added. "Enemies happen. We do our best, but they're still out there, and, God help us, somebody wanted Mason dead. That wasn't a casual shot. Somebody was deliberately trying to take him out."

"They won't succeed," she stated flatly. "No way in hell Mason would leave me right now."

Jasper half smiled at that. Mason had and always would fight damn hard to get to Tesla's side, and that wouldn't change. However, the fact remained that Mason wasn't necessarily in control right now. He had to wake up. He had to understand what the stakes were. Subconsciously he would probably know that he had been critically injured and that his team would all pitch in and help.

"Promise me," she began, her voice thick. He winced. "Don't give me any bullshit. Promise me that."

"I promise," Jasper vowed. "I promise that we will get to the bottom of this. I don't know if it will be me directing this case, but I will ensure that I am involved in some way or another."

She glanced over at him. "You haven't even had your department meeting yet, have you?"

"No, I haven't," he replied, "and they may decide that I'm too close to this case, too close to Mason. After all, we are related," he noted in a wry tone.

"I don't give a crap what they say," she snapped.

"Good, then you may want to apply some pressure yourself."

She frowned at him, then immediately pulled out her phone and started sending text messages.

"Keep in mind that you cannot come across as a *completely* overwhelmed. irrational and hysterical woman," he noted. After a moment of silence she shot him a look that had him grinning back at her. "Just checking. Not a person on base wouldn't allow you some leeway, after what you've just witnessed." He shut up under her stare.

"Doesn't matter whether they would or not," she declared, her tone determined.

"Who are you contacting?" he asked, as she went back to texting.

She shrugged. "As high up as I can go."

"Good, but what are you telling them?"

"That I want you on the case." When he sucked in his breath, she nodded. "You might not like that, but there's not much of a choice right now."

"You won't make me very popular, will you?"

"Like you give a shit about a popularity contest," she noted.

"No, I don't, and, yes, this is the work I do, so no doubt about my popularity status. However, that's not exactly the way to get started on a new base, and I don't know people here."

"Yet you seem to know Masters," she pointed out, a question in her tone.

"I knew him from way back. Plus I met him a couple days ago, when I was on base."

"Does he have any idea why you were here?"

"No, but I've come from a SEAL team that he knew, so we share mutual friends."

"Do you have a good rep or a bad one?"

"I have a *hard* rep," he clarified, yet his tone remained neutral. "I don't give a damn how they take that."

She burst out laughing at that, then immediately stopped. "God, I shouldn't be laughing at a time like this."

"Not much to laugh about right now," he agreed. "Yet, if laughter helps you to stay balanced, if it helps you to remain somewhat stable, and if it gives you a different perspective so you can handle what's coming," he shared, "then laugh. You hang on to anything that you can because, God knows, we will all need it going forward."

NURSE AMBER RACED to the ER, as the emergency call had gone out. The ambulance was just backing up, doors opening, and the hospital team already surrounding the gurney. Amber thought she recognized the face of the patient but couldn't be sure, not with so many bodies in the way. A lot of discussions were going on around her at this military hospital, with expert efficiency evident, as everybody moved to do their jobs.

Murmurs swirled around Amber, as well as the two paramedics, who gave them a rundown on the patient's condition and what had happened. Sniper rounds, two wounds for sure, possibly a third. One caused carotid bleeding. A second shot was abdominal. She winced because the head shot would be the worst and the biggest hurdle to get the patient over.

He was losing blood at a rapid rate, and they'd already called in to have a blood transfusion ready.

Amber knew all of this was good, but it would be a hell of a deal. She was called over and given a set of instructions, and she carried them out, watching the team move with the efficiency she would expect from them. When another emergency call came, she raced to join her team, where she quickly helped a pregnant woman, who had just been brought in, with complaints of contractions and vaginal bleeding. Amber winced at that one too, hoping it would be an easier fix than the other patient.

With the pregnant patient handed off to the nursing staff, Amber returned to see what the results were for the sniper shooting victim. She caught several doctors discussing it. One of the nurses stepped over to Amber and shared, "He's been sent up to surgery. He's stable. We've got transfusions happening, but that head wound is bad news."

Amber winced and nodded. "Did you hear who it was?"

The nurse shrugged. "Something about Mason. He's been here forever, and somebody apparently took him out on the base, right when he got off one of the flights."

Amber stared at her in shock. "Oh, my God." She looked around a little uneasily because, as soon as a sniper was found on base, things tended to shut down very quickly. "Have we been locked down?"

The nurse shook her head. "We haven't received any orders to that effect, but a military investigation team is coming over to hear the details on the victim's condition.

I'm glad I don't have to deal with that." She gave a mock shudder. "Some of the guys on that team will be opening a can of worms," she stated, with an eye roll and a big knowing grimace.

Amber nodded and didn't say anything. She was much more concerned about the patient and about a sniper being on base. As she waited for a call to shut down the entire hospital, she went through the frantic motions of dealing with triage in the ER for the next hour.

When she caught a moment of calm, she noted a tall, square-set male, standing off to the side, a frown on his face, his hands on his hips.

She eyed him cautiously, but, like so many of the other men on active duty here, he was fit, strong, and capable. However, this one was incredibly pissed. She walked over to him and asked, "May I help you?"

He glanced around before speaking. "A friend of mine, a family member, came in here a little bit ago, with sniper wounds."

She nodded. "Mason. He's in surgery." Clear, soft-gray eyes, with a cutting edge, caught her attention.

"Condition?" he snapped.

"Stable, but critical," she responded. "We expect an investigative team to be here very quickly. Are you part of that?"

He gave her a clipped nod. "If I can get on the damn team, I will be," he muttered. "In the meantime, I'm family, and I would like very much to have updated information, as it becomes available."

"If you contact the front desk, they'll let you know." She hesitated. "Does he have a wife, family?"

"He does, and I have his wife here." He looked behind

him. "She's pregnant and sitting down in the other room."

With that mention, Amber's mind returned to the other pregnant woman, still in the ER, where OPs and GYNs were checking her out. "Hopefully Mason will make a full recovery," she shared. "I can't imagine anything worse."

He gave an absent-minded nod, but his gaze still fully assessed the ER, and she wasn't sure what was going on here. In a low voice, she asked, "Will we lock down?"

He frowned at her. "You haven't already?"

She shook her head. "Not that we've heard."

He groaned. "I'll make a call." That being said, he quickly disappeared.

Amber stepped into the nearby waiting room, seeing him on his phone and off to the side. A pregnant woman, who Amber thought she recognized, sat off to the side, her head in her hands. Amber walked over to her and sat down beside her. "Are you waiting for an update on Mason's condition?"

The other woman brightened. "Yes, yes, please." She turned to the man on the phone.

"I just spoke to him," Amber noted, nodding. "The doctors will give you the official update, but I can tell you that Mason's in surgery. A fair bit of damage occurred to his skull, but they're hopeful they can piece it together. Now that the bleeding has stopped, the swelling is the next biggest concern," she murmured.

"Right." The pregnant woman, with a determined expression, gave Amber a half-hearted smile. "It's so hard to wait. We want answers, and we want everything now. I'm Tesla, by the way."

"I'm Amber," she replied, offering her hand. She looked over at the man who she had talked to first. "And is he family?”

“Yes,” Tesla replied, with a nod. “He’s my cousin, and he’s been staying with us. He had driven me to the airport to pick up Mason.” Tesla gave a half-gulping sob. “So, I watched my husband get shot, watched him drop,” she shared, trying hard to get a grip. “I was still so far away,” she murmured. “I couldn’t get to him in time, and then, when I did get closer, he was completely surrounded.”

Amber nodded sympathetically. “And yet those who surrounded him obviously had some combat medical training or the like and did a good job of assisting Mason, until he could be brought in.”

Tesla nodded. “Yes,” she whispered softly. “I know Masters was there and Jasper. I don’t know who all else. At any other point in time I could probably tell you exactly who was there.” Tesla blinked several times, then let out a soft groan.

Amber asked sharply, “Are you okay? Is the baby okay?”

Tesla rubbed her baby bump and nodded. “I think so. It’s just been such a shock, and the baby hasn’t accepted it that well either.”

“Of course not. The baby knows that you’re in pain and upset. So, of course, it’ll react the same as you do. You might want to take it easy.”

“Right, but there is never any good reaction in a situation like this.”

“No, there isn’t,” Amber murmured, as she looked around. “I’m on duty, so I’ll leave for now, but, if you need anything, you let me know.”

“Thank you. What was your name again?”

“I’m Amber,” she repeated, introducing herself a second time. “I’m one of the ER nurses here.”

“I appreciate any information you can share.”

"No information yet. For now, all we know is that Mason took two direct hits, and he's in surgery, where they're taking out one of the bullets. He's lost a tremendous amount of blood," she added. "Beyond that, they will deal with whatever they find during surgery."

"The second bullet?" Tesla asked hesitantly.

"Abdominal," Amber confirmed. "So a gut shot as well." She watched the color fade from Tesla's face, and Amber winced. "I'm a firm believer in family being better off knowing the truth," she shared, "but, if you want me to spare you the details, just let me know."

"No," Tesla replied. "I do not want the details sugarcoated, but obviously my condition is not the easiest. Plus, I must look after my baby as well. However, the truth I can deal with. Finding out lies and half-truths afterward would be much harder."

"Agreed. Can I get you some water or something?"

Tesla stared at her. "Hardly ER protocol."

"Don't you worry about it," Amber noted. "I want to ensure that you don't become a patient."

"Thank you," Tesla replied gratefully, "and some water would be lovely."

CHAPTER 2

AMBER QUICKLY RETURNED with water for Tesla and noted she had now been joined again by the other man. She struggled to remember his name, then it came to her. *Jasper.* Tesla had told Amber that he was family. As she handed the water to Tesla, she looked over at Jasper. "Anything?"

He nodded. "Yes, the base is on full lockdown now."

"Shouldn't that have been done already?" Amber asked.

"I think it probably was done, but the news may not have filtered out very quickly."

"Maybe," she murmured, thinking that had to be wrong. "Anyway, we haven't had any disturbance here, so it's not an issue."

"It's *always* an issue," Jasper clarified. "What we don't want is for whoever took out Mason to come here now for a second attempt."

She stared at him for a moment, then winced. "Do you think that's a possibility?"

"It's always a possibility. Those shots were well placed from a sniper atop a building hundreds of yards away."

"Oh, my God," she muttered, as she stared off in the distance. "Someone from the military then." Her voice was low.

His voice stayed equally low, as he studied her sharply and nodded. "One would expect so, with at least some good training."

Amber's eyes widened. "And yet whoever shot Mason was on base, surrounded by people, who also have had that training?"

"So, isn't that a great place to hide a lost sheep?" Jasper suggested.

She pondered his meaning and then nodded slowly. "I guess if that's what you wanted to do, that would make a whole lot more sense. You've got hundreds, if not thousands, of suspects."

"Exactly, so do me a favor. If you see anybody hanging around, anybody you don't like the look of, who isn't needed in the area, or who seems potentially troublesome in any way …" He let it hang there for a moment, then added, "Let me know."

"There hasn't been up until now," she stated hesitantly. "I only came on shift four hours ago, so I'm not sure what time frame you're looking at, but Mason was shot within the last, what? Sixty minutes?"

At that, Jasper nodded. "Exactly, but that doesn't mean somebody wasn't here beforehand, checking out the lay of the land, searching the hospital, wondering about an update on information, or looking at the layout, just in case a second attempt needs to be made."

"I can't imagine anybody with your training considering second attempts," she suggested. "You would go all-in the first time."

"All-in is the perfect situation in an op," he confirmed with firmness and a hint of disdain. "That doesn't mean a second man wasn't hanging around to check on Mason's condition when he arrived here."

"Oh, now that's a different story," she admitted, thinking back. "I had a second ambulance come in with a pregnant woman not long afterward. … As in ERs everywhere, an awful lot of chaos was happening when Mason arrived," she murmured. She frowned, thinking about who else might have been sitting in the emergency room.

"We did have a full ER waiting room," she noted, with a wince. She hesitated, then gave him a miserable look. "I can't start digging into it now, as I'm on shift. I'll keep it in mind though. Yet you may want to take a look yourself, once you get clearance," she stated. "Anybody here who's looking for assistance will go through the triage nurse."

"And yet, if they're just sitting here, with supposed friends and family, we won't know who is related and who isn't, right?"

"Unfortunately that is quite true," she replied, with a nod. "If somebody wanted to pretend to be with *the family*, they would just sit close by, and everybody else would assume that they were waiting for treatment or were somebody else's family member."

"Exactly," he agreed, nodding, as the sinking feeling settled in. "So, the question is, … was anybody just sitting with random people but not looking for treatment?"

"You mean, just looking for information?" she confirmed, her voice low, as she looked around at the full waiting room off to the side. "If that were the case, they would still be here."

"Maybe they are," Jasper stated, with half a smile. "I've been surreptitiously taking photos while I'm here, so I've caught everyone here."

She nodded. "Good. If I sense anything, I'll let you know." Just then the code alarm went off. "Got to go." And she bolted back to her station, preparing for the next emergency patient coming in by ambulance.

JASPER WATCHED AS Amber took off, racing to the ambulance doors, now opening to bring in a gurney with another patient needing help. He looked back at Tesla to watch her sipping water, huddled up in her seat. "I would love to take you home where you could rest, while you are still waiting for information, instead of keeping you here." She shot him a look, and he nodded. "That's what I expected, but anything that'll put you and the baby under further stress," he noted, "isn't a help."

"I know that," she agreed, as she considered his words. "On the other hand, if anything goes wrong with me or the baby, I'm already at the hospital."

He stared at her. "Please tell me that you didn't just say that."

"Of course I said that. Apparently another pregnant woman is already in one of these ER rooms right now, dealing with her own troubles."

"That's not the easiest thing in the world," he said.

"But forget about me. ... Why are you staying?" she asked, looking at him sideways.

He gave her a nod. "For exactly the reason I just told her." He pointed to ER Nurse Amber. "Plus, I'm not officially a part of the team yet. I also want information on Mason's condition, and I also want to know if anybody else is here."

She looked around. "You think somebody is here who may have had something to do with the attack?"

"Or is being paid to find out what condition Mason is in," he replied, carefully wording his concern, as he looked around casually. "They won't wait for the news to come out. They'll want it firsthand."

"If they've hired somebody, that's hardly firsthand."

"It may not be firsthand, but it's probably as close as the shooter would dare to get. Although, if he were incredibly confident, which I'm sure he is, given the brazen attack on base, he may be here in person."

At that, she straightened up and suggested, "We should be sitting out in the main waiting room then."

"We're just off to the side, where we can at least have conversations privately," he pointed out, "and that's what we need. Plus everybody in there has to walk right past us."

She nodded. "I didn't think of that."

"That's because you don't do what I do," he explained. "I need you to trust that I will do everything I can to get to the bottom of this."

"I do trust you, Jasper," she stated. "I just can't imagine who would have done this."

"I'm hearing that from everybody. With this Mason investigation, it won't be easy. Everybody loves him. Everybody thinks he is a great guy."

"And yet he did handle a lot of men and women, and he had to move lots of guys off his units because they just weren't good enough."

He gave her a sharp glance. "If you know that much, I'll get you a piece of paper. I need names."

She nodded. "It will give me something else to focus on, instead of what's happening to him in surgery."

Jasper walked over to the reception desk and asked the woman there for some paper and a pen, but he didn't give her much choice or a chance to argue. Spying a small notepad off to the side, he snagged it. "This will work perfectly. Do you mind?"

She shook her head and watched, as he took a pen off the counter and returned to Tesla.

As he handed her the notepad and pen, she looked back at the woman and smiled her thanks. Then she faced Jasper and asked, "Did you terrorize her for this?"

"I don't know why anybody would think I terrorize people," he stated smoothly.

"Yeah, because that's on your record."

"When interrogating witnesses, that's not terrorizing."

"You're not terrorizing me," she admitted. "However, if I weren't family, and Mason weren't involved, how you would you treat me?"

"I would treat you with respect," he declared. "I don't understand why people always have the wrong impression of me."

She giggled. "I don't think it's a wrong impression. I'm just not sure where that hard-ass attitude gets directed."

"Never at you," he declared, with a smile, "never at you." She shifted uncomfortably. He watched as she slowly placed a hand on her back, pushed her back against the chair, and closed her eyes for a moment.

When she opened them again, she caught him staring at her, and she shook her head. "Don't even think about it. I'm fine."

"Sure you are. How about a cup of tea?" he asked, almost as an afterthought.

She smiled gratefully. "That would be lovely." Then she

looked around and sagged back. "I know it's a very selfish thought, but I could use a cup."

Already in the act of getting up to see about her tea, he sat back down and asked Tesla, "What about Sebastian?" he asked quietly.

She nodded. "He's with my father," she said, with a small smile, "enjoying some grandparent time."

Jasper asked, "Have you told your father everything?"

She nodded. "I sent a text, so I am sure he's on full alert too."

"He would have been on full alert already," Jasper murmured, "because, of all the things that everybody here knows, when somebody like Mason gets shot, it puts everyone on high alert. We don't know whether assassination is the issue or something completely different."

At his use of the word *assassination*, Tesla gasped.

Jasper winced again. "See? I'm not used to sugarcoating words."

"Don't start now," she muttered. "I've always trusted you to tell me the truth, and I need that to continue."

"And that you will have." He leaned over, kissed her on the cheek, and added, "So tell me, what your gut is telling you right now?"

"If killing Mason didn't work the first time, that should make any second attempt on his life harder to do. So I would think our son's health would be in danger now. Mine too, if only to put added pressure on Mason or to use us as leverage. That alone might finish off Mason," she replied, shaking her head. "My father will protect Sebastian. However, since I'm here at the hospital, that makes me an easier target than my son. Hopefully they will come after me, not Sebastian. Plus I presume the shooter or his minions will be looking for me—

or for anybody else—waiting for an update on Mason, right?"

The fact that she had thought such a thing meant that, somewhere along the line, she considered that a possibility. "Are you not telling me something?"

"No," she said. "Maybe over the years I've gotten jaded … or overly suspicious."

"Absolutely," Jasper agreed, "as you should. So, now you're not going anywhere without me, and you'll get a guard until we get to the bottom of this."

"Oh, as if I want that," she stated in horror.

"You brought it up," he pointed out, with a smile. "And Mason will have my hide if anything happens to you and his children, born and soon to be born."

"Will you stay with me?"

"I will," he confirmed, "unless I can't be here. … So we need somebody else assigned to just look after you and to check in on Sebastian, someone we trust. But more than that, I need an investigator to help me on this." He pulled out his phone, looked down at it for a long moment.

Tesla noted, "You don't even know who to call, do you?"

"No, in many ways I don't," he admitted, "because I don't know many people in this place. I'm not sure who can and cannot be trusted. Because the shooter was on base for this attack, I am more than a little concerned about having somebody from the base involved in the sniper shooting."

"Mason has a lot of men and a lot of teams who will be here in a heartbeat, and I'm surprised that they're not here already."

"That's because the front entrance to the hospital has been shut down," Jasper explained, "and your phone's off."

She shook her head. "I didn't shut it off."

"No, but I did," he declared, relaying those words with a hard look. "The last thing you need is to be bombarded by everybody asking how you are, where Sebastian is, and the latest updates on Mason."

She pulled out her phone and stared at it blankly. "That was pretty tricky of you."

He gave her a small smile. "Not to take control, by any means," he shared, "but to limit additional contact. Only so much you can handle. With your father watching Sebastian, just focus on Mason, you, and the coming baby. Now, do you know any men I can trust here to help me in this investigation?"

"Lots," she declared, "but, if you want somebody completely not connected to this base, you mentioned Masters. He's relatively new to Mason's team. He passed Mason's good judgment, at least at the time." She smiled. "Obviously you know I can name so many people, men Mason admires and who would bend over backwards to do whatever was needed."

"I'm sure, and I'll need them as backups; but, for my investigation team, I want faces that nobody has seen or who are new to the base."

"Won't *new to the base* make them suspicious?"

He smiled. "That's true." He put away his phone. "I'm heading out for a meeting right now, and I've contacted somebody who will look after you."

She stared at him. "You're leaving now?" Her voice rose into a small squawk.

"I am because I want to get on this investigation team," he stated, "and that means, I have to go in person to make my arguments."

She just nodded. A moment later, he pointed behind her. She turned, and there, waiting in the wings, were Markus and Evan. She smiled at the two men, who acknowledged her with a dip of their heads, before they turned to study their surroundings.

"So they were already here for me, weren't they?" Tesla sighed. "As I said, Mason has easily fifty men we could call on in a situation like this."

"Yeah, and a lot of them will be put on officially," Jasper noted, "but I also need some covert people for investigations, people nobody knows and who are here unofficially, but that's my problem to solve."

"Start with Masters," she suggested, "particularly if you already know him."

"I do. I haven't seen him in years, but he was always real back then."

"I know he passed Mason's radar test because he invited him to join one of the SEAL teams."

"Good enough for me." Jasper nodded at her. "I'll contact Masters. In the meantime, Markus and Evan are your bodyguards. They will be switched out on a regular basis, so everybody is fresh. Lots of people are pretty pissed off because you're right. At the end of the day, Mason was well loved." Then he winced, realizing that he'd used past tense. "*Is* well loved," he corrected.

She gave him a haunted look. "He has to survive," she whispered.

"He will," Jasper said. "Stand firm on that. Mason won't leave you now." She nodded, but the tears were evident in the corners of her eyes.

"Go do what you can do," she whispered. "I need to know that this asshole is caught and that Mason, the baby,

Sebastian and I will be fine."

Jasper got up and walked over to where Markus leaned against one of the walls. "Two men you trust every four to six hours, set up in teams, don't care how. I'll get funding."

"You're leaving?" Markus asked.

"I'm off for a meeting right now," he shared, as the men measured him. Markus particularly studied him intently. "Yeah, you don't know me, and I don't know you," he admitted, understanding Markus's reluctance. "Tesla is my cousin. Mason and I go way back, and no way in hell I want anybody coming after Sebastian and Tesla and the baby, much less another attempt on Mason."

Markus nodded. "That ain't happening on our watch."

"Potentially somebody in the waiting room or hanging around here is looking for an update on Mason's condition and any other intel they can get. They may be blending into the crowd, as if seated among supposed family and friends," he noted. "If the job is done, maybe they are too, or they'll move on to a secondary target. And, if the job isn't done, the entire family is here right now, outside of Tesla's father, who has Sebastian. As you two probably already know, Mason's parents and his brother have passed away."

Markus nodded and surveyed the room quickly. "Where are you going?"

"I've got a meeting with the brass," Jasper shared. "I want this investigation to be mine."

Surprised, Markus asked, "Have you got the chops to make that happen?"

"Yes, if I want to force it, which right now I do," he stated succinctly. "I'm just hoping not to have to use pressure."

"Use it," Markus declared, looking at Tesla. "Nobody knows you, so you're an unknown face, who will be both suspicious and not."

"Yeah, true enough. What about Masters? Do you know him?"

"I do know him," Markus confirmed. "How do you know him?"

"From a few years back," Jasper said. "I'm hoping he's still on the straight and narrow because I need a couple people who are green here but still solid to add as investigators on my team."

Markus hesitated and then nodded. "Vet Masters," he suggested, "and, if you need somebody else, I might have a couple more names."

"Okay, I'll catch up with you in a bit," Jasper said. "First I'll get Tesla some tea, and then I've got to get to that meeting." He looked down at his phone and winced.

"I can get the tea," Evan offered.

Jasper nodded to him but said, "I'll deliver the tea. I want to ensure that she's covered. She's holding up, but then none of us would expect anything less."

"Exactly," Evan replied. "Cooper is one of our team, and his wife, Dr. Sasha Childs, is one of the doctors here."

"Seriously?"

"Yeah, she's doing a stint here, training for some specialized surgical procedure," he explained, with a wave of his hand. "I can't even tell you what the hell it's all about, but she's up in the OR right now."

"That's good to know. So can you get some inside scoop for us?"

"I'll get all the scoop I can pry out of her," he said, with a grin. "She's a straight shooter, so if something can be shared, she'll say it. She won't sugarcoat the truth."

"None of us needs sugarcoating right now," Jasper

agreed.

And, with that, he raced to the cafeteria area, grabbed a cup of tea, and picked up a little bit of food, knowing that Tesla probably wouldn't eat it, but the baby might need some nutrition.

When he rejoined Tesla, he handed her the muffin and tea. "Remember that the baby's blood sugar might need a boost."

AMBER WORKED TIRELESSLY for the next few hours, until her shift was over. She checked in with Tesla several times, brought her a little bit of food from the staff's break room and made her more tea. When she saw the woman flagging, she suggested, "I know you want to stay here, and I know that you're all about looking after Mason and making sure you stay connected to your husband. I completely understand." Still, Amber felt that Tesla needed to see reason. "He's due to come out of surgery anytime now, but you need to look after yourself, and you need to look after the baby."

Tesla blinked slowly and nodded. "I was planning on going home, as soon as I find out how he is," she murmured.

"And yet you could be at home, feet up, resting, and I could call you." She gave Tesla a reassuring smile. "You also seem to have some men keeping an eye on you." Amber's gaze wandered over at the two men standing guard. "Apparently we're still in danger."

Tesla shrugged. "Until it's solved, they will make sure that I don't become the next victim."

"Ouch." Amber frowned. "I don't want to even think of that."

Just then the surgeon walked toward them, fatigue on his face, but a somewhat cautious smile. Amber was happy to see that Dr. Charles had been on Mason's surgical team.

When Tesla struggled to rise, the doctor rushed to her side. "Don't get up," he murmured.

At that point, Amber stepped away and spoke to someone else.

The doctor took a deep breath. "Mason is out of surgery, and he's doing … okay, considering. His vitals are poor right now, but we expect them to pick up."

Tesla sighed in relief, yet Amber heard a *but* coming.

"He bled pretty heavily through the surgery," the doc explained. "So that is an issue, but we've got lots of blood for him now, and we've put out the call for more."

"Thank you."

"We can call upon lots of people on base, if necessary," he shared, "and I've been told the phone has been ringing off the wall with people who want to donate blood, so that's always a good thing."

She looked up at him gratefully. "That's very sweet. Thank you for sharing that."

"I can only tell you that, for the moment, we're cautiously optimistic," he added, "but please understand. He is definitely not out of the woods, and recovery will be slow."

"That's fine," she whispered, with a nod. "At least he's alive, and he can work at recovering. … The alternative is just too hard to even imagine."

"I understand that. Obviously it's a tough scenario, but again, we're cautiously optimistic. Now, please go on home and look after yourself."

She nodded, then slowly got up with his help. "I may run home for a bit of a break, but I need to see Mason before

I go."

"You won't see him for a few hours at least."

"Considering the severity of his wounds, I plan to stay with my husband. Can I have a cot delivered to his room?"

"Because you're pregnant, I wouldn't advise that," he replied bluntly. "I don't want a second patient."

She stared at him for a long moment. "If your wife was in that hospital room," she argued, "would you say the same thing?" When he frowned, she nodded. "Exactly, you wouldn't. If our situations were reversed, you would be camped out in her room for the duration, and you know it."

He cast a glance around the room and saw Amber. Their gazes locked for a moment, and then Amber came to Tesla's aid, promising the doctor, "I can arrange it, and I will get her to stretch out and to rest."

He frowned, not liking the idea, but Tesla was undeterred.

Amber had to admire the tenacity it took to stand her ground, especially when she was so obviously exhausted.

Tesla added, "If he doesn't make it, at least … I, I would have spent his last few minutes with him," she whispered, tears clogging up her throat. "Please don't take that away from me." The doctor opened his mouth to protest, but she shook her head. "Again, if our positions were reversed, where would you be staying the night?"

He groaned. "Fine." Then he looked at Amber, with a frustrated glance. "You will handle setting this up?"

"I will, Doctor," she stated, with a smile. "I'm off duty anyway."

At that, Tesla turned and said, "No, in that case you need to go home."

Amber shook her head. "I'm not going anywhere. We're

in lockdown. Remember? Just give me a minute and let me go find out which room Mason's been assigned to. Once they've got him moved in and settled, I'll arrange to get another bed in there for you."

Tesla smiled and nodded. "Somehow I'm sure it will work out."

"However," the doctor interjected, "the minute you become a patient, all deals are off."

"Got it." She smiled up at the doctor. "Thank you."

Shrugging in resignation, he muttered, "This is against my medical advice."

"Objections noted," Tesla murmured. "You and I both know that I need to do this."

He sighed. "I hope your husband is half as stubborn as you are," he grumbled. "It will bode well for his recovery."

Tesla burst into laughter at that, and the doc even grinned back at her. "And thank you for that laugh. I hadn't realized how much I needed the relief and the chance to breathe."

"That's part of the problem with you hanging around the hospital," the doc pointed out. "The stress and this tension is not good for you. You'll put yourself into early labor, and we'll have two of you here, with a newborn in the nursery or an incubator."

"If it happens, it happens," Tesla declared, "but not because I'm not looking after myself. So let me go lie down on a bed beside my husband, and I will work whatever mumbo-jumbo magic I can dream up. You've done your part, for which I am very thankful. Now let me get in there and let him know that I'm here for him."

"Pretty sure he knows already," the doc replied. "Tesla is your name, I presume."

"It is, but why do you say that?"

"Because he was hollering about *looking after Tesla* every time he surfaced. I kept telling him that we would do just that and that he needed to focus on getting better, so he could take over the job. That seemed to calm him down."

"He probably thought he was dying," she whispered.

"Oh, I imagine he was, and I can't guarantee that he isn't. However, it is a good sign, with that head injury of his, that he remembers you and that he called you by name." And, with that, he nodded to the two women and left.

Amber held up one hand and addressed Tesla. "Give me a few minutes." And, with that, Amber quickly walked over to find out what room Mason was being transferred to. With that done, she headed up to check the status of the preparation of his room in the ICU. As she strode to the room, the attending nurse frowned. "It's already been cleared with the doctor and promised," Amber shared. "Plus, she's pregnant."

"Oh *great*. So what then? You think we need another patient to look after?" Amber just waited for the nurse to blow off some steam. The attending nurse sighed. "Fine, whatever. You know the rules as well as I do."

"I do, but, if we can get a cot in here, Tesla promised that she'll be quiet as a mouse in the corner."

At that, the other nurse rolled her eyes. "Sure, until chaos erupts, and she's in the way, and we need to move her."

"If that's the case, we move her, and that's the consequence of being right here on the spot. You and I both know that, if our husbands were in ICU, we would be here too."

The other nurse winced and nodded. "Unfortunately I had to be here for mine not all that long ago, so I hear you, and that's fine. Just give us a few minutes to get the patient set up."

"Will you bring in a cot, or do you want me to handle it?"

"We'll deal with it," she offered, "just give us some time." And, with that, she turned and walked away.

Amber waited until Mason was brought in and settled. Then, once everybody had given him a full check of his vitals and his wounds, the orderlies brought in a cot. She smiled her thanks at them, and they quickly disappeared. She studied the layout of the room, happy a private room with a bathroom had been assigned, which included a little bit of extra space, where they could hopefully get Tesla set up in a fairly comfortable way.

And, with that, Amber returned to the ER waiting area and smiled at Tesla. "Let's go." She noted the relief on the Tesla's face, as she slowly got up, and they moved to the ICU, along with her two bodyguards. "You might have fooled the doctor, but you haven't fooled me. You're in a lot of physical pain, and we can't have that."

"I won't lose my baby," she declared. "Pain? Yes, but mostly because of that damn chair."

Amber nodded. "You're right. The chairs in the waiting rooms are not geared for people to sit in very long. Unfortunately sometimes people must stay way longer than we would like them to. Reducing the wait times in the ER would be a lovely thing. We had been doing pretty well, but then, with COVID and the usual ER chaos affecting staffing, it's become a problem again. We'll need to take another look at it," she noted. "Like the rest of the country, we've been dealing with staffing shortages right along with a host of other problems. So, considering all that, I suppose we should be grateful that we have what we have."

"I, for one, am grateful," Tesla said, "particularly knowing that Mason is alive."

"He's alive but still in danger."

"Yeah, well, it seems like we all are in danger at the moment."

At that, Amber asked sharply, "Don't suppose you've heard any update on that?"

"No, nothing. You know the way this stuff works," Tesla murmured, taking a moment. "We're not likely to get an update until it's already over."

"In that case, let's keep you close to your husband. I presume your security duo will remain nearby as well?"

"Yes, they will be here in pairs in rotating shifts. However, I'm more concerned about making sure that somebody is here for my husband. Obviously I'm staying, but if a gunman were to come in, ... I'm not exactly in the best position to argue."

Amber laughed at her. "You may say that, but I highly suspect that a mama tiger like you won't let anybody get close to her husband."

"Normally that's very true," she said, with a smirk. "Just not right now, not after this emotional trauma and the physical drain on my body. I'm not quite in fighting shape at the moment. However, when push comes to shove, I would definitely do my very best."

"I have no doubt about that," Amber agreed, as she pushed open the ICU door and ushered Tesla in. "The current nurses on this shift have been alerted that you're coming, but they're also worried about you being pregnant during this stay with your husband. They don't want you to end up as a patient yourself, so they'll be quite concerned about your condition."

"I'm pregnant, not fragile, and I am quite capable of

looking after myself," Tesla declared. "I just want to be as close to Mason as I can be."

And, with that, Amber led her to the area where Mason had just been settled, noting the two men following in their wake.

As Tesla walked inside Mason's hospital room, she stopped, her hand going to her mouth.

Amber stepped up beside her. "You can hold his hand, but please don't move his arm or any of the tubing in any way."

Tesla whispered, "I promise. I do want to hold his hand though."

"You can kiss him too, but he's hooked up to an awful lot of critical wires and tubes right now. So I need you to be extra careful that he is not unplugged from any of them."

"I'll be careful," Tesla promised, tears pooling in her eyes.

Amber winced. "I'm not being hard on you. I'm just out on a bit of a limb here."

"I appreciate that so much," Tesla muttered, without even looking at her. "And I don't mind your being hard on me. I'm a lost wife and a devastated partner, so my brain isn't working as it should. Thus I appreciate any attempt to keep me on track."

Surprised at that response, Amber replied, "Too bad everybody doesn't feel that way."

Tesla shot her a look and then nodded. "We're never at our best when we're up against something like this," she admitted, "and I appreciate everything you've done to keep things moving in the way I want them to."

Amber added, "After seeing what Mason's been through and has survived so far, I don't see any reason why his condition won't improve, especially knowing you're here. I believe that patients *do* know we're there. So remember that when you're spending time with him. Talk to him—tell him to rest and heal, tell him that you're here, tell him that you love him."

Tesla chuckled. "Yeah, he'll probably be quite irate at the idea of me thinking that he needs to rest, when he's always been a power machine."

"And he will be again," Amber reassured her. "Don't forget that, no matter how tough it gets."

"Thank you." She looked over at Amber with a smile. "It's so much easier to face this when you have all that confidence."

"I've been in this medical world for a very long time, and I've seen patients like Mason before. We need to give him as much of a chance as we can to survive, despite how bad it might look. We can never count him out because he has the power and the ability to surprise us. I can already see Mason is like that," she shared. "So you continue to talk to him, and we'll do our best to look after him."

And, with that, Amber pointed to the cot tucked in the corner, as well as the three-drawer chest and the closet nearby. "Get somebody to bring you whatever you need to be a little more comfortable," she suggested. "I'll arrange to get some meals brought in for you."

When Tesla argued, Amber shrugged. "No, it's not my department, but that's okay. I can help and will, as much as I can, but you need to do as I ask and take care of yourself. So, go spend a minute talking to Mason, give him a kiss without disturbing his tubes and monitors, then lay down and have a nap."

"I know. I know," she muttered, with a nod.

Between the oxygen tubes, the drainage tubes, and the IVs, Mason was hooked up to machines that beeped and whirred all around them. Tesla's eyes filled with tears at the sight of him. "Looking at him like this is a shock, yet I am so thankful that he is alive."

Knowing the emotional and physical pain Tesla was in broke Amber's heart, but she also had to remember how strong this woman was and that she had the ability to survive this, no matter what happened. They all wanted a positive outcome, but certainly had no guarantee.

She'd seen Mason upon his arrival. Amber had seen cases that seemed to be absolutely no problem yet turned completely ugly in a very short time. And she had seen dire circumstances work out into miraculous healings. As soon as she was sure that Tesla would rest and relax, Amber added, "I'll leave you for now, but don't hesitate to ask for help." And, with that, she quickly left.

As she stopped at the open door and looked back, Tesla stood there, holding Mason's hand, tears streaming down her cheeks, as she softly spoke to him. Amber smiled because she knew that the power of love was absolutely unmatchable when it came to healing. Mason appeared to have a massive team behind him, but the biggest thing he had going for him was the woman standing at his side.

JASPER WALKED OUT of the department meeting and pumped his fist in success. He made it back outside to his vehicle and found Masters standing there, waiting for him.

"And?" Masters asked.

"And what?"

"Did you get on the team?"

"I did," Jasper confirmed, "although I'll be operating independently."

Masters stared at him for a long moment. "What the hell does that mean?"

"I think they're planning on doing a couple arms in this investigation."

"Are you sure they didn't just tell you that so you could feel like you were doing something?"

Jasper stopped for a moment and frowned. "That would suck."

"It would also be typical brass."

"Maybe," Jasper conceded, taking a moment to let go of the sting. "Either way, I won't let it get to me. Believe me that I'll be diving into this investigation in a big way."

"And it would be stupid of the brass to ignore your skills," Masters noted in that studiously quiet tone.

At that, Jasper turned to look at him. "What does that mean?"

Masters raised an eyebrow and shrugged. "I've kept track of you over the years."

"Why did you do that?"

"Because you're settled into an interesting field that I also considered."

"Investigative work?"

"Yeah, I didn't want to ever investigate our own people, but, if ever an avenue outside of that came up," he shared, "I must admit I find it very interesting."

"I did very specialized jobs," Jasper explained, "so, yes, you're right. The brass would be foolish not to take advantage of my skills, but I acknowledge there's a lack of trust on both sides," he admitted.

"Of course there is. They're the brass, and this sniper shooting happened on their turf, and you're new, so nobody'll want you here."

"And yet you're new yourself, aren't you?"

"New enough that I recognize the challenges you'll face."

Jasper laughed. "Yeah, I can see that. On the other hand, I don't give a shit," he declared. "I'll get the answers I need, … for Tesla's sake, if nothing else."

"You guys are close, *huh*?" Masters asked, as he stepped up beside him, while they walked over to Jasper's car.

"We are, and I was in rough shape after one of my jobs finished not all that long ago. The two of them were there for me. I don't know another man I respect more than Mason. So to see some asshole do this to him does not make me happy."

"That's good to know," Masters noted, with a smile, "because none of us wanted to see that happen."

"Having a man down is one thing, but having a man down and being happy about it is a whole different story."

As they approached Jasper's truck, he hit the key fob to unlock it, turned to look back at Masters, and asked, "What are you doing over the next few days?"

Masters crossed his arms and declared, "Helping you."

Jasper frowned. "How do you think that'll work?"

"We'll see, but I owe Mason too."

"Sounds like half the base does."

"Maybe, but I'm the most recent addition to his team," Masters shared, "and I'm not impressed with somebody taking away from me the opportunity to work with Mason."

Jasper considered the man before him for a long moment and then nodded. "In that case you better hop in."

"Where are we going?" Masters asked, as he walked

around and got in on the other side of the truck.

"We have a couple things to check out, but one of the first is knowing exactly where the sniper was and what skill it took to make that shot."

"I know the building because I've already been up there." When Jasper raised one eyebrow, Masters shrugged. "You were looking after Tesla, and the ambulance had left with Mason. So I was free to take a look at the spot myself."

"Good, in that case you can show it to me. Did you get any insights?"

"Highly skilled is how I would call it. Wind was going crosscurrent, plus a tricky shot already, which is probably why Mason's still alive."

Jasper nodded. "That was my take too. *Bastard.*"

"Yeah, I'm glad we're on the same page with that one."

"Now the next thing I want to know is whether this is something that's just targeting Mason, or is it more widespread?"

"We won't know that, not until we find out more."

"I'll agree with you there too," Jasper agreed, "but we'll also have a problem finding people who will talk. Everybody loves Mason, but nobody'll know anything about this."

"You think they will all go silent?"

"Not sure if it will be so much going silent as not understanding motive. This was a pro job."

"As in a professional hit?"

"I wouldn't be surprised, and neither will I be surprised if somebody who once was here at Coronado, who knows the lay of the land, had already scoped it out. Somebody who knew what would make the biggest bang for the buck and how close the hospital was. Even more than somebody who just would have done some online research. I think this was somebody who spent a lot of time here, but I would also hazard a guess that he's not active here anymore, so somebody who's gone private."

Masters thought about that for a moment and then nodded. "Works for me."

"That'll make it that much harder to find him."

"Not necessarily, if you can get Tesla to give you a hand," Masters noted, with a sideway look. "Presumably you have some influence in that quarter. You can have her do a rundown of anybody who's been here and is now gone."

"Yeah, I was planning on it," Jasper stated. "I've already got her making a handwritten list of any potential suspects, people who didn't make the cut to be on his team and the like. I'll head back to the hospital and take her a laptop as soon as we get a few things done. She'll appreciate working on the computer instead of on paper. She's only thinking about Mason just now. However, as soon as she gets a chance to see him, and her brain wakes up a little, she'll realize she can do something here to help us investigate. So her help in this investigation will make a huge difference. That'll give her a purpose and something else to focus on."

"Exactly," Masters agreed. "In that case let's go take a look at the sniper's nest."

It took them only a few minutes to get to the base of the building in question. As they arrived, several other men hung around. Jasper noted each one of them, then, ignoring them, he walked into the building. Nobody stopped him; nobody even made an attempt to stop them or to ask for credentials. He just shook his head at that.

Masters snorted. "I guess nobody has any idea what the hell they're doing, do they?"

"Seems so, except they're all expecting the investigation

team to sort it out."

"*A team* will sort it out," he murmured. "I just don't think they realize who the hell is on that team."

At that, Jasper laughed out loud. They quickly moved inside and, taking the stairwell, they headed up to the roof. With Masters at his side, the two men stood atop the roof and surveyed the angle that the shooter would have shot from. As it was, they had a bird's-eye view.

"Honest to God, there couldn't be a more perfect sniper position than here," Jasper noted ruefully.

"And yet the plane ... could have pulled over somewhere else."

At that, Jasper turned and asked, "Are you saying the pilot's in on it?"

"No, I'm not saying that at all," Masters clarified, "but it's definitely something I would want to look into a little bit."

"It could have just been good timing and wonderful positioning."

"It's possible," he acknowledged, "but you know we don't like to leave things to fate."

"No, we sure as hell don't," Jasper muttered. With his eyes narrowed, he studied the distance, the current winds, and then turned back to Masters. "Best case, it's still a damn tricky shot, with a moving target, the possibility of a different landing spot, the wind at any given second, the number of others on the tarmac. Even with a silencer, people will notice when someone goes down, especially once blood is evident."

"And, if the sniper didn't make the kill shot, how would he correct the problem?"

"At this distance, he may have been able to make two or

three attempts, if the first didn't do the job."

"But what we know is that he made one good attempt to kill Mason, in that Mason went down, and the shooter had surprise on his side back then, where he might not have another chance."

"He still got off two shots," Jasper stated, turning to look at Masters.

"Right, he did get two off, so the second one was probably … rapid fire, two shots pulled fast, both good hits, each could possibly kill him. Yet neither were fatal, and that's the problem right there."

"I presume his motive was an assassination, and, in order to make something like that work, he needed it to be fatal."

"Both shots weren't fatal, and I'm damn grateful for it," Masters muttered.

"You and me both, but right now we have a problem."

He acknowledged that with a nod. "That we do."

"What are the chances any cameras around here were pointed at the exact spot on the tarmac where Mason got hit?"

"This entire base should be covered in cameras, but what do you want to bet there won't be one single functional camera that we need to look at—or not one covering this particular area?"

"That's the next thing." Jasper pulled out his phone and took a sequence of snapshots of the area for him to peruse later.

Masters nodded. "It's almost like you're thinking about taking a shot yourself."

"No, but I do want to know what else the sniper had for choices, and this way I have memorized the scene. You know this base a little better than I do."

"Not by much," Masters replied, with a shrug. "I've been here a whole two weeks longer than you."

Jasper frowned at him. "Oh, is that all?"

He nodded. "Yeah, that's all. I was looking forward to the next step, joining Mason's team. Meanwhile I had been doing some investigative work and was torn on continuing to do that."

"You'll get that chance to learn from Mason," Jasper declared. "We just need to get Mason back on his feet."

"If that's even possible."

Jasper frowned. "You're damn right it's possible, and we're not talking about any other alternative."

"Got it," Masters said, with a grin. "I can see why Tesla likes you so much."

"She doesn't have much choice," Jasper noted, with a half laugh. "We're family."

And, with that, he led the way back downstairs.

CHAPTER 4

AMBER RETURNED TO the hospital for her next shift. She'd spent half her night calling in periodically to confirm that Mason would be okay. She wasn't so sure why she was so concerned over Mason's case, above all the other hospital patients, but she was. Maybe seeing Tesla waiting so desperately for news, yet Amber routinely saw people equally as caught up in their own situations.

Just a fact of life when working in the ER. Some cases went just fine, and others you couldn't do anything for. She'd seen so much of that. As she walked down the hallway, she was surprised to see the man she'd first seen with Tesla. *Jasper.* His name was as unforgettable as his face and those mesmerizing gray eyes.

He noted her approach, then frowned, and she frowned right back at him. Oddly enough that brought a smile to his face. "Hey. It's Amber, right? I wanted to thank you for looking after Tesla."

She shook her head. "I don't need thanks for that. Tesla is in a very delicate position right now, and I don't want to see anything happen to her." She didn't come out and say something might happen concerning the pregnancy, but what she meant was obvious.

He nodded. "She mentioned how kind you've been."

"You've seen her already this morning, then?" she asked.

He nodded. "Yes, and Mason made it through the night, so we'll take that as a good sign."

"Absolutely," she murmured. "Anytime a critical patient makes it through the night, … that's a huge bonus."

"And that's how we'll look at it too," he stated, with a smile. As she went to move past him, he reached out an arm.

"What?" she asked.

"Did you get a chance to think about what I asked you—about somebody suspicious in the waiting room?"

"Oh, yes," she replied, the confusion leaving her face. "I did think about it. I can't say that I came up with anything or anyone specifically, but hard not to think about it, once you mentioned it."

"Yeah, life is like that," he agreed. "Yet I don't want you looking at everybody sideways."

"Are you sure?" she asked in a dry tone. "It seems to be exactly what you're looking for and what I was doing."

"No, not at all," he murmured, "but I do want to ensure both Mason and Tesla remain safe."

"I'm going on my shift now. I planned to stop in to see her before I started, and then I'll check in with her a little bit later."

"And, if you see anything odd, anything that's weird, different, or the slightest bit strange, let me know." She hesitated, and he knew right away what that was about. "And, yes, I'm now officially part of the investigation into Mason's shooting."

She nodded. "Okay, that makes me feel better."

"It's amazing how people need to have that official status."

"Aside from HIPAA regulations and privacy concerns, it's not even that," she clarified. "In reality, for all I know, *you*'re the one who shot him." He stopped, shocked. She shrugged. "Hey, I don't know you. I don't know anything about you," she pointed out bluntly. "So, the fact that you want information like that identifies you as somebody who is possibly a little too interested."

"That's a good way to look at it," he murmured, staring off in the distance, before returning his attention to her. "So, if anybody else asks you, maybe you could keep that in mind and let me know."

"Will do."

He pulled out his phone. "This is my number."

He quickly gave it to her, and she added it to her Contacts list, then stared down at it. "That's not a local number, is it?"

"No, I've just come out West," he told her.

"So, you haven't been staying with Tesla very long then," she said, trying and failing badly to keep the note of suspicion out of her tone.

"Not very long, no," he agreed, with half a smile, "but I've been here for several weeks, months even, I guess. I was recovering from an injury myself." She couldn't help but sweep a glance over him. "I'm in fine shape now, but I do understand what Mason must be going through."

"How long were you down?" she asked, curious now.

"Too damn long if you ask me. On the other hand, it does change your perspective about your work, as well as your life, and what you choose to do with it."

"That I can understand." She nodded. "I'm glad you're back on your feet."

"I'm back and fighting for him, and don't ever think

anything else," he stated, with a light warning in his tone. She smiled. "Anyway, if you do hear or see anything, let me know, will you?"

She nodded, then watched as he quickly left. As she walked over to hang up her sweater and to put away her purse, one of the nurses pointed at Jasper's quickly disappearing form.

"Wow, you got nice and close to him," the nurse shared, a note of envy in her words.

Amber frowned at Andrea. "I don't know about that," she replied, with a laugh.

"If you don't want him, send him my way," Andrea stated. "That's definitely hubba-hubba material there."

And, with that, Amber burst into laughter and headed down the hallway. Still pondering Andrea's comment, Amber made a quick trip to check on Mason and Tesla. Amber had done a little bit of research on the pair overnight, when she'd had a moment, and had been quite surprised to see just how much was out there.

Tesla herself was incredibly well respected and apparently did one hell of a job with computer systems. As Amber walked into Mason's room, Tesla worked on a laptop, resting on her cot, leaning up against the wall at the head of her bed.

She looked up when Amber walked in. "There you are," she greeted her, with a smile. "I wasn't sure whether you were working today or not."

"Four days on, four off," Amber shared, "and I only get the four off if people don't go making a mess of their lives."

Tesla nodded. "That can't be easy."

Amber noted Tesla's very calm demeanor and how she looked much better. "I gather Mason is doing well?"

"He held on through the night, and I know Mason. If he

can make it through that, … he can make it through anything."

"That's excellent news."

"I know that he'll be just fine," Tesla declared, with a bright smile, "and I certainly won't waste my time bemoaning the fact that he's hurt. I would much rather spend every moment I have doing what I can to make his world a whole lot easier."

"What is it you think you can do to achieve that?" Amber asked.

"I don't know yet, but I'll figure it out," Tesla replied. "Jasper was looking for you. Did you see him?"

"I saw him as I came in," she said. "He's very determined, isn't he?"

"He is, indeed." Tesla laughed. "So, whatever it is that he wants, you might as well just give it to him. Otherwise he'll hound you until you do."

Amber grinned. "No surprise there. He does appear to have that dedication."

"That is one way to put it." Tesla smiled. "Yet he's trustworthy, and we've been best friends as well as cousins for a very long time."

"I was surprised he hasn't been here all that long."

"No, not this trip. I wanted him to come when he first started to heal, but he didn't want to be a burden," she explained, with an eye roll. "And now that I don't want to be a burden, he still won't listen to me."

Amber chuckled. "It goes along with being an alpha male, I think."

"It does, but anyway, as you can see, I'm doing much better today, so you don't need to worry."

"I'm not sure that *worry* is quite the right word for what

I was feeling," Amber stated, "but I am happy to see that you and Mason are both doing better. Now, did you get some breakfast or tea?"

She nodded. "Yes, I had tea earlier, and breakfast should be coming soon. I am a bit tired now, but I promise I will have a nap as soon as I need to crash," she pointed out. "Don't worry. Jasper has already been all over me about it."

"Good," Amber said. "I'm in full support of that."

"Of course." Tesla wrinkled up her nose. "Everybody likes to hound the poor preggo lady."

Amber grinned. "And I'm pretty sure you can use that to your advantage anytime you like, only listening to others when you feel like it."

Tesla burst out laughing and then quickly lowered the volume, as she looked over at her husband. "That is very true," she admitted. "I think it's something that we all do."

"I wouldn't be at all surprised," Amber murmured. "Anyway, I'm heading off to start my shift, if you don't need anything."

Tesla smiled and shook her head. "I'm good, thank you."

"If you do need me, do you know how to get a hold of me?"

"Since you're down in the ER, I presume it's pretty easy to locate you."

"It can be, but at times it can also be a little bit more difficult than you think," she explained, as she jotted down her number and handed it over. "If you ever need me, don't hesitate to call."

"Thank you," Tesla replied. "Everybody here has been wonderful to deal with."

"Good," Amber said. "We aim to please." She started

out the doorway and then looked back at Tesla. "There is also a cafeteria, so, if you feel like you want or need something better or different, you can always go down there."

"Good to know. I hate admitting this, but, anytime I think about getting up to go for a walk, I stop and think about how far away everything is and decide that maybe I'll sit tight."

"Good to know, but I can always have something sent over for you, if needed."

"I'm fine for the moment. Go to work before you get in trouble. I'm thinking I might just shut this down for a bit and have a nap."

"A nap is not a bad idea," Amber agreed in a warm tone. "You've got to look after that baby."

"So everybody keeps telling me." Tesla chuckled. "Personally I think this baby is doing just fine."

"And that's how we want to keep it," Amber noted, as Tesla rolled her eyes and smiled back at her.

With that, Amber turned and walked toward the ER. As she got to her floor and headed to her station to check what was happening so far, she heard people talking in the nearby waiting room. She cast a glance back and saw two men, speaking in low voices.

One of them turned and glared at her.

She turned away, wondering what his problem was. When it came to ER rooms, there were often private discussions about patient care, who needed what, and what they would do about paperwork, payments, and so forth, so she wasn't at all surprised to get that reaction from someone.

She thought about it, as she walked over to the front desk. She thought she'd seen the angry man before. She walked into her ER section to ensure everything was ready and up-to-date, when one of the nurses stopped her.

"Hey, are you okay?" she whispered.

"Yeah, I'm fine. Why?"

"That guy over there is staring at you," she shared, "and I can't say it's a nice look."

Amber turned, knowing exactly which man her coworker was talking about. And, sure enough, he was glaring in her direction. She stopped and studied him for a moment, wondering if he would turn away, but instead he seemed to be even more belligerent about it. She shrugged. "I don't even know who he is."

"I don't like the look on his face," the nurse shared, "so watch your back."

Amber winced. "That's the last thing we need around here."

"I know, right?"

"Not as if we don't have enough headaches to worry about," Amber muttered, "but he doesn't look friendly at all."

"Did you walk in on a conversation or something?"

"Or something. Yeah, just as I was walking in, the two of them were having one of those, you know, deep conversations."

"Right, like the ones that we're always told to look out for? The ones about arranging signatures when they're not allowed to and power of attorney and all that good stuff."

"Yeah, except I didn't get that feel from it."

"Good, can't say I want to go up against those guys. Something is very dodgy about both of them." And, with that, the nurse took off.

Amber thought about it for a long moment, then pulled out her phone and walked past, holding up her phone as if checking for messages, while casually taking a video of both their faces as she walked by, not knowing why she was doing it and wondering whether this was even legal. Still, Jasper had told her to keep track of anybody slightly suspicious in her book and how it could help him. And although that angry reaction wasn't all that suspicious, it wouldn't exactly clear the angry man of suspicion either.

Not to mention that she had seen at least one of them yesterday.

She walked right on past and quickly sent the video to Jasper. She forgot about it for a couple hours, as the ER picked up, and she had several patients to work with. Once things calmed down a little bit again, she took a deep breath, brushed her hair back, and turned when someone called out her name, as a triage nurse came to her.

"Somebody's on line one for you."

She picked up line one, half recognizing the caller's voice.

He only spoke two words. "Call me." Then he disconnected.

Not sure why he didn't just call her on her cell, she pulled out her phone and sent Jasper a text. **Was that you?**

When she got a **Yes** back, she called him and stepped outside of the hospital in the back, where a little smoking corner was. A couple people in the corner puffed away, so Amber stood off to the other side, where she didn't have to get inundated with the smoke herself. "Why, and why this way?"

"Just seemed better."

"If you say so. What do you want?"

"Why did you send that video?"

"Oh, I'd forgotten all about that. Just that they reacted

oddly when I came upon them this morning, and their conversation seemed a little *suspicious*. Now, before you ask, … no, I didn't hear what was said. They just shut up all at once and glared at me. Plus just something about them I didn't like, and I think I had seen both of them before—yesterday, I believe—although I definitely saw the larger bald one yesterday."

"At the ER?" Jasper asked, his tone sharp.

"Yes, at the ER, and, yeah, a lot of that day."

"Interesting. Have you checked on Mason and Tesla recently?"

"Not since I first arrived." Then she froze, asking in a careful tone, "Should I?"

"I haven't been able to get back there. I know that she's still under guard, as is Mason," he shared, "so I'm sure they are fine."

"Now that you have mentioned that, I'm about to go on break, so I'm heading up there right now," Amber offered. She walked back inside the hospital and stepped into the elevator, choosing the correct floor.

"I don't want you to panic her or to make her feel like something is wrong."

"Then you tell me. Is something wrong?"

"No," Jasper stated. "I don't think so, but, when you sent me that video, I wasn't sure what to think."

"Right, and I'm not much help because I don't know why I even sent it to you, except that I'm apparently being paranoid."

He chuckled. "In this case, it's appreciated. Better paranoid than having a problem we're too late to fix."

"That's what I was thinking, until you questioned me about it." She groaned. She walked over to the room, now that she was on the right floor, then looked through the window in the door. "Tesla is in there napping," she shared. "Do you want me to go in and disturb her?"

"No, not at all, but can you tell that much through the window? You know, to be sure that she's sleeping?"

"She's curled up in a fetal position with a blanket over her, right at Mason's side." She turned, looked around, and saw one of the military men she'd noted yesterday. "One of the men you set up yesterday as a guard is here."

"Describe him," he ordered, and his tone brooked absolutely no argument. She quickly described the man as best she could, and she heard an audible sigh. "Good, that's Markus. Nobody would get past him."

"You still think there's a problem, don't you?"

"Yeah, I do." And, with that, he ended the call.

JASPER HEADED BACK to the tiny room he'd been assigned as an office on base and requested access to cameras, hitting roadblocks. All part of the special team request apparently, and, if he wanted access, he would have to go get it through them. He frowned at that, wondering whether anybody even knew that he had been given special access to this case or if he would be up against a roadblock there as well. Time would tell, and he wasn't at all sure what he would find down that road. Nevertheless it wouldn't matter one way or the other, as he would be a part of this, regardless of anybody else's interpretation of right or wrong.

He walked down the hallway to the other rooms he assumed the rest of the team occupied but wasn't exactly sure. Poking his head into a couple of them, he realized that the entire space appeared to be empty. Continuing to the main front desk, he asked the receptionist who was in charge of the Mason investigation.

She shrugged. "There's a team, but I don't know who is involved."

"That's fine, as long as my name is on it."

She stared at him steadily. "I don't know who you are, so I don't know if it is or not."

His lips twitched at her deadpan delivery and nodded. "Good point," he replied, with a smile, knowing the benefits of laying on the charm when he chose to. "I'm Jasper Maclintok."

She nodded. "You're the latest name that was just penciled in."

"I'll take that to mean yes, so I'm a full-fledged member of the team," he stated coldly.

She raised an eyebrow at his tone, but he didn't give an inch. The last thing he wanted anybody to think was that he was short of a fully functioning member in this case. At that cold stare that didn't stop, she gave him the room number, where the team was assembled. He nodded, then turned and headed for them, wondering why everything always had to be so difficult. What was the need for so much secrecy all the time, and, all too often, far-too-much secrecy that excluded the wrong people.

He couldn't do the job if he didn't have access to information. He understood that nobody would be particularly happy with his involvement, since he was an unknown factor, who nobody knew. The current investigation team would struggle with that. The investigators would be people who knew Mason, knew of the base, not somebody who came in out from the cold. Jasper also understood that to a certain extent, or at least he understood enough that he wouldn't sit here and let it bother him. And, once they found out he was family, they would get him off the case anyway, but that just wouldn't work for Jasper.

He did have some pull, though it might all be from back East, but he had it. As he walked into the room, silence came. Jasper noted four men, and he nodded, quickly introduced himself. Several people looked from one side to the other, and, with a hand raised and his tone cool, Jasper declared, "In case you haven't gotten the memo, I'm part of the team."

Heads turned to look at one man, who Jasper assumed would be leading the investigation. He raised an eyebrow in a questioning manner. "I presume you've been told?"

"We have," the head man confirmed, his tone easy but his gaze watchful. "We're just not sure how you managed to get onto an investigation team when you're clearly new to the base."

"I'm new to the base but not new to investigations. I'm certainly not new to betrayals, and I'm not new to problems inside a base," Jasper declared. "So, in this case, although I might be new to the people here, I can come at it from a very different perspective."

"And is it a fair perspective? We know the people on base." This investigator also came on strong.

"That's right. You do know the people. At least some of you will know some of the people," Jasper corrected. "I'm not here to step on toes, but this is what I do, and this is what I did back East. So, while I'm new here, I'm not new at all."

A long moment passed, while everybody assessed his words, and then the man in charge spoke, with a scrutinizing gaze. "It's not as if I have any way to argue with you or to tell you to get the hell out," he admitted, with a smirk, "which I would do in a heartbeat if I thought it would work."

"Save your energy. It won't," Jasper declared.

"I assumed as much, so the only thing I can say is welcome to the team. Expect to get some hard looks your way because we don't know who you are."

"That's fine, and there will be hard looks going both ways, until I can clear people on this base from being involved in the assassination attempt on Mason." When several of the men sucked in their breath, Jasper nodded. "No way that every person on this base is not a suspect right now. From the first moment Mason took that hit, that had to be on every damn mind here."

"What's your connection to Mason?"

He raised an eyebrow. "Tesla is my cousin," he shared. "I'm the one who shut down the hospital an hour later than it should have been done. I arranged for the guards at the hospital, and you can bet we'll all be taking shifts, making sure that Mason is well taken care of."

"Obviously everybody on the base wants the best for Mason," one of the men said coolly. "So it won't go down well if you start accusing all of us too."

"I don't give a damn what goes down well." Jasper refused to turn and look at the person who had just spoken. Keeping his hard gaze on the team leader, Jasper added, "My only concerns are catching whoever did this and ensuring nobody has a chance to go after Tesla." A rumbling came all around him, as he turned to look around the room from one investigator to the next. "Please don't tell me not one of you considered that."

"No reason to think that she's in any danger," the head

man replied. "However, it is something that I had wondered and had brought up with the brass."

"I have too, and funding is in progress to cover the security," Jasper shared. "Now, introductions, please."

They all looked at each other, and then the leader began, "I'm Morgan. To your right is Sam, and you've got Lichen on the other side of you. Steve makes up the fourth, but he's on medical leave, yet popped in to say hi."

"I'm Jasper. Nice to meet you all."

"Is it, or will you sit there and do a full check on us first?" Sam spouted off.

"I would be very derelict in my duties if I didn't," Jasper replied. "So considering that's one of the things you brought up right away, let's just deal with that first." Sam may have been sarcastic, but Jasper wouldn't pass up on the opportunity. "Where were all of you at the time of the sniper shooting?"

Shocked silence followed, as they all frowned at each other.

Jasper shrugged. "No way we aren't having this discussion. So it's your choice. Either here and now in front of everybody or later in private."

Morgan spoke up first. "I was at the hospital, visiting a friend. I had to sign in, and I'm sure multiple people saw me."

"Were you there when the ambulance arrived?"

"I was, but I didn't know it carried Mason, not until a little bit later," he shared. "Maybe fifteen minutes after the incident, we were called in to gather information."

At that, Jasper turned to look at Sam.

"I was home with my wife," he replied in exasperation. "Is this necessary?"

"If it weren't, I wouldn't be asking," Jasper declared. "And your wife can verify that? Anybody else?"

"My wife is hardly someone who wouldn't be considered trustworthy."

"I don't particularly like husband-and-wife alibis," Jasper noted. "So, if anybody else saw you, it would be a lot more helpful."

Sam shut his jaw and glared at him. "I was talking to my team within a few minutes of that," he added. "So I can give you the names and the people I talked to, if you want to verify my location at the time," he bit off.

"Thank you, that would be appreciated."

Sam stared at him in shock. "You're serious, aren't you?"

"You damn-well better believe it." Jasper turned to look at Lichen. "Unusual name," he noted calmly.

"Yeah, it is, but that's all right. I'm used to those comments," Lichen shared. "And where was I? I was training, and you can speak with the armory personnel. I signed in, and I signed out. Unfortunately I was one of the last to hear about Mason."

"The armory didn't hear?"

"If they did, they weren't passing it on, but we were all doing some pretty intensive training," he explained, with a shrug. "You know what that's like. Nothing stops until you complete it."

Jasper nodded. "Give me the times in an email, will you?" He handed out his email address, so that everybody could send him their information in writing. Then he looked over at Steve, who was sitting back, his legs crossed and up on the table. "And where were you at the time?"

"Oh, I'll answer, but I also want to know where the hell you were."

"Good. I'll answer that as soon as you answer my question." Jasper didn't give him any quarter on it.

"Where were you at the time of Mason's shooting?"

"Jeez, I can't believe that you suspect any of us," Sam sneered.

Jasper didn't take his gaze off Steve. Steve would be a tough nut to crack.

"I was in the offices here," Steve shared, with an attitude. "I have a fair number of reports that I'm getting caught up on before I leave," he muttered.

"So, did you sign in and sign out that day?"

He hesitated and then replied in the same condescending tone. "I avoid signing in and signing out as much as I can, so I'm not sure that I did."

"What is your reason for avoiding that?"

"Because I don't always want people to know where I am," he admitted. "It's damn hard to get work done if they can come in and find you at any time."

Morgan rolled his eyes. "Damn it, Steve. We've gone over this. You know you're supposed to sign in all the time."

"Of course I know that," he snapped. "And obviously, if I would have known somebody had just been shot, and I needed an alibi, that's the first thing I would have done."

"But, in the meantime, you don't have an alibi," Jasper noted.

Steve stared at him for a long moment. "I'm not sure that I do. What will you do about it?"

"Keep you on the suspect list," Jasper declared, still giving no quarter. "So, therefore, I won't be sharing any information with you, and I will request that you be taken off the investigation team for this case, which, if you're truly on medical leave, you have no business being here now as it is."

CHAPTER 5

TESLA WOKE SLOWLY, her back aching and her belly bouncing with the baby's antics going on inside. It took her a moment to realize where she was and to remember the horrible situation they were in. She shifted, stifling a groan, and walked the two feet over to Mason's bedside, where she once again leaned over, kissed him on the forehead, and whispered into his ear, "I'm still here. I will always be here, and, when you're ready to come back to the world of the living, I will be here too."

Checking his color with a wary eye, she noted that he was still holding steady. While no sign of consciousness appeared, he didn't seem to be any worse either.

She made a slow waddling trip to the bathroom, as she rubbed her aching back. When she came back out, a nurse stood off to the side, checking the machines.

"How is he doing?" Tesla asked.

The nurse turned, with a smile, and replied, "He's holding on."

"Which is as good as we can expect right now, I suppose."

"Honestly I'm delighted he's holding because that's a huge sign. The doctors are deliberately keeping him under right now."

At that, Tesla nodded. "I figured."

"We don't want him to be awake and in pain," she explained. "So, let's get him through the recovery period after surgery, keep his vitals stable, and we'll all be in a much stronger position to see where he's at. The fact that he came through the night so well is a positive thing. Huge."

And, with that, she did a few more checks, while Tesla watched. It had always fascinated her to see the medical world going on around her, but she'd never been so keenly aware of every move and how incredibly vulnerable they all were when they were in the hospital. Unconscious as Mason was, anybody could do anything they wanted to hurt him, and that thought was just unbearable.

Tesla hovered constantly, not getting in the way, but slyly taking videos and images to ensure that, if anything did go wrong, she had proof of who may have had something to do with it. She didn't have enough knowledge of what was happening and what the nurses were doing to feel comfortable enough with their actions. Tesla didn't think she would ever get to the point of being comfortable with that.

Right now, Mason was at the mercy of everyone, which is why Tesla wouldn't dare take her gaze off anything.

When the nurse was done, she smiled at her and asked, "Now, what about you?" She eyed Tesla critically. "Did you get any sleep last night?"

"I did," she replied, "but you don't need to worry about me. It's all about Mason."

"Yes, Mason is definitely our priority," she confirmed comfortably, "but none of us want to see you in a hospital bed beside him."

She winced at that. "Neither do I," she admitted. "I need

to be here for him the whole time."

"Which is why we need you to take care of yourself," she replied, with a motion at the cot. "I'll get somebody in to change the sheets. Did you get any clothes brought over for you?"

"Not yet, I'll make that arrangement today." The nurse frowned at her, and she shrugged. "I'm not leaving Mason."

"He's doing better, so you could go home and get some clothing and maybe a bite to eat or something to make you feel better."

Tesla just shook her head. "No, not happening."

The nurse stared at her for a moment and then shrugged. "Maybe I understand that too." And, with that, she was gone.

Tesla stared after her, as she returned to her cot and sat down again. It might just kill her to be here because that cot was anything but comfortable, but the thought of leaving Mason at anybody's mercy when he was in his greatest need was not something she could ever do.

When the door opened and Evan walked in, he smiled at her and held out what looked to be coffee. "I wasn't sure how much coffee you're drinking with the baby."

"Definitely one cup a day," she admitted, "and I probably shouldn't have more than that, but it's pretty-darn hard, under the circumstances."

"I can always get tea," he offered.

She smiled up at him. "Thank you for caring so much."

"Mason is our friend and don't ever doubt that we're here for any other reason than his benefit. And yours," he added, as an afterthought.

She chuckled. "I did hear the afterthought in that."

"No, at least it wasn't meant to be." He grinned bashfully. "Obviously we're all concerned about both of you."

"Thank you for that too," she replied, with a nod. She settled back a little on the cot, as he handed her the cup he had brought over for her.

"You don't want to go home? You can't be very comfortable here."

"No, it's not comfortable at all," she shared, "but that doesn't matter. I'll be content here, as long as I'm with Mason." And her tone brooked absolutely no argument.

He smiled at Tesla. "And Dr. Sasha Childs… or Sasha to us, was in the OR with Mason. She'll stop in to talk to you, when she gets out of another surgery she's involved in."

"She was part of his surgery?" Tesla asked with muted hope.

He nodded. "She was called in as an extra because they were short on hands."

"I'm glad to hear that," Tesla shared warmly. "It makes me feel much better, knowing that she was there and looking after him."

"She was hoping you wouldn't mind."

"God no," she replied. "It does show you how loved Mason is, with all that I'm hearing from people around here."

"Very loved," Evan confirmed, with a gentle smile, "but along with that love comes the opposite. Somebody out there doesn't love him at all."

"I know. I've been racking my brain, thinking who that could be," she admitted. "I just can't think of anybody in his work or in his personal life who would hate him this much."

"There's also the chance that somebody here was hired for the hit," he suggested.

She nodded. "I know, and, for that reason alone, every time a nurse comes in, I'm watching like a hawk," she shared, "and I know that I'm probably not allowed to, so it's completely illegal, but I'm videotaping absolutely everything they do to Mason."

He nodded with approval. "That's not a bad idea, and the fact is, if you are keeping such a close watch, it will slow down anybody looking to make a second move on him."

"I can only hope. I'm hardly much of a threat, and I'm sure people would look at me almost comically," she conceded, "but I'll make damn sure that, if anything happens to him, I'll have some proof of it. I'm so frustrated that I know so little about the medical processes that he's already undergone and could be undergoing again. Even when the nurses come in, I find myself questioning if they need to be doing what they're doing or if somebody else will get at Mason."

Evan walked over, sat down on the cot beside her, picked up her hand, and shared, "In that case, when my wife, Megan, comes in later, tell her that. Explain to her what you want to know more about, so, if somebody is up to something, you'll be aware of what to watch for."

"Oh, that's a good idea," she agreed, looking at him. "I could do some research on it too."

He shook his head furiously. "You'll just get tons of messed-up and even contradictory information," he pointed out, standing his ground. "Let Megan tell you, and then, if you do see something that raises your suspicion, you'll make an informed decision as to whom you need to contact. We all know how incredibly talented you are," he added, "so let's put that to good use right now, while we're here. You are his number one primary watchdog, and we are the security outside."

"Are you still standing watch outside?" she asked, staring

at the door behind him.

"I have been, and now we have somebody else to take the next shift."

"Who is it?" she asked warily.

At that, he let out a sharp whistle—which Mason slept right through—and Corey poked his head around the door.

She smiled up at him. "Hey, I'm so glad to know who's out there."

"About sixteen of us signed up," Corey shared, "so don't you worry. It will all be people you know, all people you can trust."

With tears in her eyes, she nodded, as Corey stepped back out again. She looked over at Evan. "Thank you," she whispered.

He smiled, patted her hand. "You don't need to thank us. You know we love Mason, and we love you, so we'll do everything in our power to get to the bottom of this. I know that it's an upsetting thing to talk about, but I do need to ask you a few things."

She took a deep, calming breath and tried to stabilize the chaotic emotions whirling through her and nodded. "Of course. Go ahead."

"Did you see anything?"

She shook her head. "He had just arrived, and I was getting to him as fast as I could, but I was anything but fast," she admitted, with a smile, patting her tummy. "I was so excited to see him, and I heard something. Then I saw the red all over him, as he stood still for a moment. I just froze. I was in shock, not quite understanding what had happened, and then I heard that noise again, almost … sounded like *pew, pew,*" she explained, imitating the sound. "The noises came very close together, which I hadn't expected, I hadn't expected any shots, so I don't know what I'm talking about."

She pinched the bridge of her nose and groaned. "This is enough to make you crazy."

"That's fine. You're doing just fine," Evan reassured her. "So, you saw the blood appear, and Mason slowly collapsed. Is that correct?"

She nodded. "He slowly sank to the ground, and then he just dropped. Before I got there, I think the pilot and a couple other people had already been all over him. Masters was there too." She thought back to the scene and shuddered.

"Right, and do you know if Masters was on that flight, or do you know if he had any purpose for being close by?"

She shook her head. "I don't know. I presumed he was already at the hangar or something."

"Right." Evan considered that.

"That is possible, right?"

"Of course it is. That's quite possible. I'll talk to him about it."

"You should also probably talk to my cousin."

"Jasper, yes. He's already making waves," he shared, with a twitch of his lips.

"He's good at that," she noted, with a smirk. "He's been to hell and back, but I know he would go the distance all over again for Mason."

"Any particular reason?"

She hesitated and then shrugged. "At one point in time Jasper was pretty down and upset over a case early on in his career, where he ended up arresting a very good friend," she shared. "Mason was the one who helped him step out of that guilt to see that it wasn't his fault. His friend was at fault for making the choices he had. Plus Jasper still had a sworn duty to do right by the job, and that sometimes doing right by the job felt like doing wrong by the people you cared about."

"So, Mason and Jasper were good?"

"More than that. I know that back then Jasper struggled, and again in a more recent investigation, but, after talking to Mason each time, Jasper seemed to find a certain amount of peace with it; and they've been very close ever since. Jasper's my cousin and has been in my life a very long time, and we've been close. So having Mason be a part of that was an easy transition for all of us," she murmured.

"Of course. It's a good thing Mason trusts Jasper because we're all in the position of having to trust him now."

She looked up at him, nodded, and very carefully added, "If you have any other ideas, please don't. You can trust Jasper. I can't emphasize enough how important he has been to multiple other cases, cases that he was given because he would do the right thing, regardless of the outcome, yet cases that hurt him badly," she explained, with a nod. "That's one of the reasons why he delayed starting here. He just needed time to …" She broke up as she thought about it, then tilted her head. "I guess the easiest answer is he needed time to heal. His spirit was hurting."

Evan sat back and nodded. "I think, in many ways, we've all been there."

"Exactly, and Mason was damn glad to have him out here with us, so we can spend time together and could do things with him. Jasper's a good guy."

"Is he single?" Evan asked curiously.

She winced. "He was engaged to somebody in the military back East, but, as it turned out, … that was one of the people he ended up recently having to arrest."

Evan sucked back his breath. "Shit."

"Yes, a betrayal at all levels," she noted, "particularly since one of the reasons the relationship even started was apparently for her to keep him at a distance and, therefore, prevent him from finding out the truth."

"Which makes it even harder, of course. … I get that. You never want to be duped into a relationship, but to be intentionally duped into a relationship as part of a larger plan to prevent you from discovering a crime, that's a whole different level of betrayal."

"Exactly," she agreed, with a smile. "Jasper is a good guy. Don't forget that."

MASON SHIFTED IN whatever cotton-batting world he was in. He kept turning, twisting, and looking for the danger that was ever present, that the voice at the back of his head kept warning him about. *Move, move, move, now*, and yet nothing moved.

The more he tried to shift, the more he tried to get away from whatever danger was oncoming, the more he realized that absolutely nothing was moving. He couldn't move his arms. He couldn't move his legs, and somehow he was a prisoner or subdued in some way. He couldn't figure it out, and the harder he tried, the more exhausted he became, and, just as he fought off one wave of panic, another wave would come in.

He felt the pinch of something into his arm, and, for the first time, it occurred to him that maybe he was being drugged. With that thought alone, he slipped back under again. Along with the drugs went the will to fight, as he slid back into the unconscious state he'd found himself in earlier.

All the fight went out of him, and he crashed back under.

CHAPTER 6

A MBER GOT OFF for lunch at noon, hoping to run some errands, but first she headed up to check on Tesla. When she got there, Tesla was on the phone but appeared to be doing fine. So, checking to ensure that everything was well with Mason, Amber stepped back out into the hallway and headed down to her car. She was tired, hadn't had a great night's sleep, envisioning men in her ER room who didn't belong there, intent on causing all kinds of chaos. Of course she'd seen way too much in life not to realize just what chaos they could cause, and that was the last thing that she needed in her world right now.

As she got to her car, distracted and still thinking about Mason and everything that had gone on, she pulled out her keys to buzz the vehicle open. Just as she went to do that, another vehicle raced up beside her. She heard the roar of the engine, and she turned and belatedly jumped out of the way. Still, the car slammed into her hip and sent her tumbling.

Several people nearby shouted and raced toward Amber; then, she was checked over quickly. She struggled to her feet, surprised that she had full mobility, even more surprised that she hadn't blacked out. She was pretty sure she wasn't badly injured, but she was hurt and knew that she would be stiff and sore at best. Now that the shock was wearing off, she was beyond angry.

She didn't understand whether she had just been the victim of an accident, with some fool going too fast, or there was something much more ominous about it. One of the doctors she knew well eyed her critically.

"Come on. We need you back inside," Dr. Charles said, wrapping his arm around her. "Let's get that checked out."

She took several tentative steps, leaning on him, and shook her head. "I'm fine. You know it as well as I do," she muttered, "but I'll be damn sore."

"Yeah, you're not kidding," he agreed, "but I would still feel better if we got you checked out."

She frowned, but the doctor wouldn't take no for an answer. Realizing her reluctance was probably because she didn't want a fuss made over her, intellectually she still knew that this wasn't the time to argue. She went back into the ER, wincing with pain at every step. Her team raced over to ask what had happened, and Dr. Charles gave them the rundown.

"This guy just came out of nowhere and slammed into her and kept right on going," he shared, urgently raising a hand to keep them all from hovering over her. "We need to run some X-rays and confirm nothing worse is going on in there."

It took another two hours for everybody to decide that, other than the horrific swelling, bruising, and the fact that it would take days to recuperate from this, she needed bed rest. Maybe even an overnight stay. She had nothing broken, so, for the most part, it would all be soft tissue damage.

She managed to convince everybody to let her go home on the promise that she would check in with them later.

And, with that agreed to, she and a few of the medical team went back outside, walking with her to her vehicle. When she tried to get into the driver's seat, she found the pain was bad enough that she had to bite it back, just so they didn't stop her from leaving.

Then her door swung open wide, and Jasper barked, "Don't even get in on the driver's side. Let's put you on the other side or in the back seat, and I'll drive you home." When she opened her mouth to protest, he just glared at her. She snorted. "So, who died and made you boss?"

"The good thing is, *you* didn't die," he declared, "but we'll have a talk about that."

Her mouth snapped shut, and she stared at him mutely for a moment. Then, with his help, she managed to get around to the far side of her vehicle and sat down in the passenger seat, wincing at the pain still radiating through her body.

He nodded his thanks to her coworkers and got in the driver's seat. "Not to worry. I'll keep an eye on her."

There were a few grins, but a couple people seemed worried.

As soon as he started the car and pulled out of the parking lot, she looked over at him. "Are you saying this is connected?"

He looked over at her. "Did anybody see you take that video?"

She frowned but knew he was right to ask that question. "I don't think so."

"You don't think so, but you don't know for sure, do you?"

"No," she admitted, her voice dropping, as she realized that was a possibility. "I made it look like I wasn't."

"And *trying*," he noted, with a raised brow, "probably made it look like you were. Every time we hide something, it's amazing how much it ends up bringing attention instead."

"Crap," she muttered softly.

"Now, tell me exactly what happened today."

Marshaling her thoughts, she went quiet for a moment and then gave him a brief version of what had happened. "Honestly it happened so fast that I didn't get a chance to see anything."

"Which might be a good thing in a way," he replied, with a nod. "You did fall, right?"

"Yes, I did."

"Do you think the driver would have seen that?"

"If he looked in his rearview mirror, he would have had to," she said, thinking about it. "Why do you seem happy about that?"

"We want him to think that you're hurt. If he was intent on killing you, we want him to think he succeeded."

"Crap," she muttered, staring at him in shock. "Why would you even put that out there?"

"What do you want me to do? *Not* tell you?" Twisting in his seat, he faced her. "You took videos of two guys who were suspicious to you in the ER. I presume you had no chance to see who was driving the car that hit you."

She shook her head. "No, … it was totally unexpected. It happened too damn fast."

"Exactly, so we have you taking videos of suspicious guys in the ER, and now you're the victim of a hit-and-run in the parking lot. Were you here on your day off?" he asked, frowning at her. "Your shift's not over now, is it?"

"No, I planned to run some errands on my lunch break,"

she shared. "I came out to my vehicle, still debating as to whether I would have enough time. As I hit the button to unlock the door, the next thing I know, all hell breaks loose. I jumped out of the way but still got hit and ended up on the ground."

"Right, so how would somebody know about your schedule?"

She shook her head. "Only somebody who works there."

"Or somebody who can get online, I presume?"

"Sure," she said cautiously, "but that's not exactly information that anybody can just grab."

"And yet it probably wouldn't be very hard to get," he stated, with a note of humor in his tone.

She winced. "Yeah, that would be the case for people like you."

"But think about where you live and where you work," he declared, raising one eyebrow. "On this base, all kinds of people know how to do all kinds of things. In many cases that's what we're trained for."

She sank against her seat, shaking inside. Not how she expected her day to go. She had never dreamed that something like this could happen, and the thought that it could have been deliberate was enough to make her vomit. Almost immediately she yelled out, "Pull over." He pulled to the shoulder, as she opened the passenger door and heaved.

She stumbled out, and he came around to help her. When she was done, she looked up at him. "God, I don't even want to think about that."

He nodded grimly. "You might not," he noted, with a firm tone of voice, "but I have to think about it. So, if this is connected, you now need to be under guard. If there's a connection between you and what happened to Mason, I need to know what that is."

"Only the fact that I took that video," she murmured.

"Have you been seen going into Mason's room?"

She frowned. "I don't … I mean … Anybody could have seen me, I guess," she replied. "I'm just walking into a hospital room. It's my job."

"Exactly. So somebody sees you taking videos. Somebody sees you going in and out of the hospital room where Mason is being treated for an attempted assassination," he shared, looking at her calmly. "That is not a far-fetched theory to say the least. So, now we've got to consider just what is the purpose of taking you out."

"I don't know, but they didn't succeed."

He nodded, helping her to get back in the vehicle again. "Which brings me to the next point. If he didn't succeed, will he try again?"

Her head dropped back against the headrest. She whispered, "Damn, I don't even want to think about that."

"Maybe not," he agreed, "but we can't let this slide. That was a deliberate rundown, I imagine."

"If you say so."

"I do say so, and, if it wasn't deliberate, you would think they would have stopped to see if you were okay. I presume you hit the car with a pretty good *thunk*?"

She winced. "I certainly felt a *thunk* but it doesn't mean they heard one."

He laughed. "They would have heard it, and they would have been mentally measuring it, seeing just how much of an impact they'd made."

"He wasn't going all that fast," she noted cautiously. "I just thought it was an accident. It could have just been an accident," she repeated lamely.

"Yeah, maybe an accident," he mumbled, "and, then again, I'm not big on accidents." She glared at him, and he smiled. "The good news is that you're alive, that you're okay, and that we're now in a position to ensure it doesn't happen again."

"What are you envisioning that to look like?" she asked, her words sliding out, as she stared at him in shock. "Because no way I can have a guard on me. I've got to go to work," she replied, now panicking. "That's just not how this stuff works. I'm nothing to them."

"You were nothing until you took that video," he stated.

She frowned at him. "Oh, so now I'm to blame?"

"No," he countered. "I am."

JASPER NOTED HOW Amber hadn't said a word since he'd made that statement about him being to blame, but he could see that starting to build in her head, and she would want more of an explanation. Moments later he pulled up outside her apartment.

"I know it's a lot to ask, but don't start hollering about how I knew where you live. When you told me that you had taken this video, I did some due diligence to gather some facts in terms of where you live and whatnot," he explained.

She just shook her head, not believing him.

He smiled, looking at her intently. "Now let's get you up to your apartment." He came around to her side and slowly helped her straighten out. He could see the beads of sweat on her forehead. "Did they give you a pain shot?"

"They gave me a muscle relaxant and a bit of a painkiller," she admitted, "but, because I was driving, I couldn't take very much."

He didn't say anything, knowing that any painkillers could affect her after something like this, but the emotional trauma was also something she would struggle with. With him at her side, he slowly got her up to her second-floor apartment. As they walked in, she looked around and noted, "Everything here appears to be normal."

"Good, and I'm sorry you even had to consider that."

She stared at him. "I don't want to consider it. I don't want anything to do with any of this."

"And yet …"

"Right, and yet I brought it on myself," she muttered. "Crap, what the hell was I thinking?"

"You weren't, and that's why it's my fault." He got her into the living room, where he eased her into a chair. He quickly brought over a footstool too. "Let me know if it's better with or without this." She tried it with her injured leg elevated, then paled, and he removed it to ease back the pressure. "That's not better."

"No, it isn't." She grimaced. "I don't know where you get off thinking this is your fault," she muttered, "but it isn't."

"I told you to keep an eye out for suspicious characters," he noted. "If I hadn't, you wouldn't have thought to take that video."

She stared at him, dumbfounded. "I never even considered that, but it's hardly your fault. They looked suspicious. regardless of what happened to Mason," she shared.

He laughed. "You can be as mad as hell at me because I am."

"It doesn't help to be mad," she murmured. "All I want right now is to have this all go away."

"You and me both," he agreed, "but it looks as if we're in for a whole lot more than we thought."

"*Great*," she muttered.

He came back with a glass of water and stated, "I'll put on the teakettle. Better take some of your pain meds."

She closed her eyes for a moment, then opened them and sighed. "No, I don't think I can just yet. I will when this painkiller runs out."

He nodded. "I'm okay to do whatever it is you say you need," he shared. "You're the one who knows what you've taken, but don't forget that you threw up shortly afterward. Now, do you want tea?"

She smiled, then nodded. "A cup of tea would be lovely. Now you're reminding me that's what I kept giving Tesla. Although I'm starting to crash now, just as the adrenaline's wearing off."

He chuckled. "In some cases, tea does appear to be the answer. Not always, and not for everyone, but it has some magical properties, and it fixes everything."

"I wish it did fix everything," Amber muttered, her words slurring. He turned back to check on her, to see that she'd dropped her head back against the chair. He walked over, studied her for a moment, and continued to talk, but she didn't respond. With a smile, he grabbed a blanket from the back of the couch and covered her up. She never moved a muscle.

Unplugging the teakettle, he stepped off to the side, checking the entire apartment to ensure he had absolutely no reason to worry—something he should have done right off the bat, but a little hard to do without raising her suspicions.

As soon as he had that done, he stepped onto the little balcony in back and took a good look at the situation. Of course she was only on the second floor, which was still very accessible if someone with any skills wanted to get in. That didn't make him happy, and again something he would have to fix. He made a quick phone call to Morgan. When Morgan answered the phone, he explained what had just happened, which was met with silence for a long moment.

"Are you saying it's connected?" Morgan asked.

"I'm not saying it's connected, but I am saying that it's something we have to consider."

"Why did she take videos of these guys?"

"Because she thought they looked suspicious. Then she forwarded it to me."

"Did you look into them?"

"Not yet. I was just about to do that now. I can send you a copy."

"Do that," Morgan said, his tone harsh. "If this is getting bigger, and they're taking out associated targets, we'll have to put a stop to this before we have an uncontrollable amount of casualties here." He took a moment and asked in a much harsher tone, "Are you the one who told her to look out for anything?"

"I warned her to keep an eye out," Jasper confessed. "I just asked whether she had seen anybody hanging around who didn't appear to be with somebody who belonged there at the hospital, and if so, to let me know."

"Still …"

The note of censure in his tone made Jasper's back go up, and he recognized a level of responsibility here that he could get nailed over, and that was fine. He was quite prepared to accept any blame coming his way, and the last thing he wanted was to see an innocent person getting mixed up in this, but it appeared that Amber already was.

"Whether I'm responsible for her doing this or not," Jasper pointed out in a cold tone, "the bottom line is that she has been the victim of a hit-and-run. She couldn't identify anyone in the vehicle—apparently a small gray sedan. So, if we can get into the cameras for the hospital, we might pinpoint who it is."

"Anything else?"

"No, just that. At least if we can do that much, we would have left no stone unturned. Then we can knock this off the list as a possibly connected event."

"I'm on it," Morgan replied, his tone crisp. "Keep an eye on her."

And, with that, Jasper hung up. Keeping an eye on her was something he was planning on doing, but he would need to figure out his next step from here.

When Sam phoned a little bit later, he didn't sound happy at all. "Morgan just told us what happened," he began. "Do you think it's connected?"

"I don't know whether it's connected or not," Jasper admitted. "All I can tell you is that nobody at the hospital could identify the vehicle, and it happened so fast that Amber was knocked off her feet with a good-enough *thunk* that several people came running because they heard it, and the vehicle took off at top speed."

"That's not much to go on."

"That's true. Now it could have just been some asshole afraid of being charged, so he took off. Who knows? But what I do know is that, here at her apartment, she is definitely vulnerable, if somebody chooses to come back again. And the only reason I know why anybody would give a crap is because she took that video today."

"I get that she's worried, and everybody at the hospital is

worried," Sam noted in exasperation, "but the last thing we need is people taking videos."

"Oh, I hear you," Jasper agreed, "but she apparently thought someone was acting suspiciously."

"Did she give it to you?"

"Yes. I've already forwarded to Morgan, but I can send it to you as well, if you want."

"Yeah, send it along," he replied. "We should upload it to the central files anyway. That way it will be there for all eyes, and we can all do a check on it."

"We should also be pulling the cameras from the hospital parking lot, and I already mentioned that to Morgan," Jasper noted. "We need to know if anything there will help to pinpoint the vehicle."

"You stay where you are. I'll check in with Morgan."

As Jasper hung up, he noted that, in both cases, the men were basically telling him to stay put, and they would handle things. If they thought that was a way to keep him out of the investigation, that wouldn't happen. However, having her videoing some suspicious types only complicated things— unless she had found something or had triggered something, which he tended to believe. In that case maybe her actions would not be in vain, ... providing they could keep her safe.

AMBER WOKE WITH a start, jolting upright, then cried out in pain and collapsed back down. Instantly a face loomed over hers. She recognized Jasper and groaned. "Good Lord, I hadn't considered what it would be like to wake up to this."

"I imagine you're sore as hell," he replied. She glared at him, and he smiled. "I get it. You want the world to suffer, just like you," he guessed, with the same bright tone, "but I would just as soon not, thanks."

That brought a chuckle out of her. "Didn't you promise me some tea?" she asked, scrubbing her face.

"Yeah," he agreed, studying her.

She could sense the intensity of that gaze. "What?" she asked, as she dropped her hands from her face. "Am I covered in something?"

"No, but you'll need a hand to get to the washroom."

"Oh God." She winced. "That'll be painful, won't it?"

"It could be. I just don't know if you'll be difficult about the infringement, you know, on your privacy and all."

"Oh, I'll be difficult," she declared, and then sighed. "Yet I get it. This is the stuff I do on a daily basis. It's just not what is done to me."

"I hear you," he replied, with a gentle smile and a deep breath. "But, first off, let's see how you are when you're vertical. Then see if we can get you to walk to the bathroom on your own."

"Oh, I should be able to walk there on my own," she stated, "at least I hope so." With his help she managed to get on her feet, though it took a few minutes of hanging on to him for the room to stop swaying. "Good Lord," she muttered, then gasped for air.

"I know. I was hoping it wouldn't be quite so bad for you, but you did get pitched around pretty hard."

"If you say so," she muttered. "I don't have any experience to compare it to."

He smiled at her. "I understand that. Let's just keep heading for the bathroom."

And, with his assistance, she slowly made it to the bathroom door and then smiled. "The good news is, I can take it from here on my own."

"That is good news," he repeated, but his gaze was watchful.

"I'm fine," she said, waving him off. "You don't have to look after me, wondering if I'm about to collapse."

"And yet you might be, so don't worry about me. Just go in there and take care of business. If you need a hand, call out, and I'll come help."

"That won't happen."

He laughed. "If I hear somebody drop, and it sounds like you fell down, I'll be in there, whether you like it or not."

Glaring at him, while knowing he meant it, she stepped into the bathroom, shut the door, and hobbled her way over to the toilet. She used the facilities, and, by the time she was back up and washing her hands, she felt sweat trickling down her back. The pain was incredible. She opened the door, and he stepped forward.

"I can see from your face just how bad the pain is."

With her next step, she gasped. Instead of her hobbling over to the couch, he swung her up in his arms and carried her there. She cried out in amazement. "I don't think I've been carried since I was like four years old," she muttered.

"I definitely don't want you falling, and you look definitely pickled."

"*Pickled?*" she murmured. "Is that a word?"

He grinned. "I'm not sure if it is or not, but it's the one I used." He settled her on the couch, so she could stretch out. When she did, she winced in pain. Jasper asked, "Now, where are we at for the pain protocol?"

She waited a few moments, thought about it. "Grab my purse and some water, will you?" She shook her head under his glare and retorted, "I can take my own medication." She pointed to her purse, which he retrieved for her.

After she swallowed the pills, he added, "You don't have to be independent all the time. You know that, right?"

"I kind of do, because, even when you rely on people, it's sometimes hard. You expect them to be there, and sometimes they just aren't."

He nodded, totally getting where she was coming from. "Sounds like probably a story is in there."

She shook her head. "No story, just what I've learned from watching people."

"Meaning that people aren't always looking out for others?"

"Something like that," she murmured. "Like sometimes patients are stuck in a hospital bed, waiting for people to come and pick them up, or to come and visit, and they just don't show up. It breaks my heart to see people let down by someone they thought they could count on, and it happens all the time."

He nodded. "How about that cup of tea?"

"I would love a cup of tea," she muttered, as she settled back down, pulling the blanket up over her shoulders.

"Are you cold?"

"Not cold so much, but vulnerable somehow. I think I'm just feeling that way from being injured," she murmured.

"Give me a second, and I'll get a cup of hot tea for you." He quickly left, heading into the kitchen.

She presumed that, while she had been out cold, he had made himself at home, and that was a strange feeling. She hadn't had a relationship, at least not the solid long-term type in a couple years. So, when that one had broken off, the painful feelings had been intense. She had sworn off long-term relationships soon afterward. It made for a very lonely lifestyle, if that's what she would stick to, and, as it was, it hadn't stuck all that well.

She tried hard, but being lonely wasn't something she was good at. Still, she didn't have anybody in her world now and hadn't for a fair bit, so having somebody walk around her apartment was a novelty, a strange feeling. It made her realize how isolated she had become over the last few years. But hadn't everybody?

That worldwide virus had changed things so much for so many people, including her. She'd been on the frontlines for a lot of it, seeing several of her coworkers die, succumbing to the disease, and many other medical workers had gone down the same path. She had been blessed herself. She had gotten COVID but had survived, and now here she was—in this new normal, which was something else entirely.

It didn't seem very normal at all, and that was the problem. A lot was wrong with this version of normal, but it was all she had. As she sat here, listening to Jasper tinkering in her kitchen, it made her realize just how much she wanted a change in her world and how much she needed to take control of her own destiny. If this was what her world would be, she needed to raise the bar and create more of a life for herself, before something like this took her out.

She hadn't even had a chance to live yet, as far as she was concerned, and there had to be much more out there. There just had to be. The thought that somebody may have intentionally tried to cut her life short was devastating.

She had always considered herself a nice person, and now it seemed as if somebody had done this on purpose. They had deliberately run her down, not caring whether she survived or not, meaning they placed no value on her life.

When Jasper came back out, carrying a cup of tea, she smiled because he had brought along a cup for him too. "Are you a tea drinker?" she asked in a teasing tone.

"Not necessarily a tea drinker most days," he admitted, "but, hey, I can go with the flow."

"Coffee is in there," she murmured.

"I saw it, and I was tempted."

"Why didn't you just make some?"

"If I'd known you would wake up soon, I probably would have. In the meantime, I am totally okay to have tea with you." And he sat down beside her, placing both cups on the coffee table.

She replied, "I'm not sure I could have brought out one cup right now, much less two."

"You don't have to," he said, looking at her. "I'm not going anywhere."

She froze. "You're not staying here, are you?" she asked incredulously.

One eyebrow raised, he asked, "Do you have somebody else you can call?"

She flushed. "What does that mean?" she asked, keeping the anger and the fear out of her tone, as he assessed her expression for a long moment.

"That's why I'm staying."

"Good God." She got flustered. "I don't need that level of care."

"No, and that's good," he stated. "If you don't need it, you don't need it, and I'll be bored the whole time."

"That may very well be, but you can't possibly stay with me," she said. "You have to solve this problem with Mason."

"That's definitely part of what I'm doing," he shared.

"I'll start collating all my notes, and the rest of my team is looking at the hospital parking lot camera footage."

"I didn't even think of that."

He smiled, then nodded. "That's one of the reasons why we're good at what we do, so you'll stay here and relax."

"Will you start being bossy already?" she asked, glaring at him.

"I can already tell that you won't be a good patient," he noted, his lips kicking up at the corners.

And damn if that didn't do something to her insides. She blamed the shock over the whole situation, plus the drugs she had taken, because no way she would fall for some guy who was obviously so very capable and in charge. Two people that way in the same relationship would never work out as a long-term thing. On the other hand, who said it had to be long-term?

A lot could be said for a nice roll in the hay, and yet her mind argued right back, *That's not what you want. That's not the relationship you're looking for.* She gave her head a shake, only to realize he was watching her.

"Problems?" he asked, one eyebrow raised.

She flushed bright red and shook her head. "No, I'm fine."

But that gaze of his stayed intense, as he studied her. Finally he eased back and asked, "If there is a problem, you'll tell me, right?"

"Not likely," she muttered.

He straightened and glared at her. "And that"—he pointed at her face—"needs to change and fast because I can't have you holding stuff back from me, particularly if it'll affect your safety."

"I don't know anything," she declared, frowning at him.

"I haven't done anything and don't know anything. As far as I'm concerned, this was just a freak accident."

"I hope it was," he replied, "because then we wouldn't have to worry about you."

"You don't have to worry about me anyway," she stated, glaring at him. He just smiled, prompting a sharp retort. "What's that smile for?"

"Because you're getting contrary."

"I am not."

"You are, very much so."

Staring at him, she suddenly realized how silly and childish she must sound. Sagging back, she mumbled, "Fine, I'm just being childish."

He nodded. "The tea is probably cool enough for you to drink now."

She picked up the cup and sipped it, letting the tea soothe her. The warm liquid slid down her throat, like sand sucking up the first rain. "I hadn't realized I was so parched," she muttered.

He nodded. "Sometimes it's the drugs, and shock can do that as well."

She contemplated that and then nodded. "Sounds as if you've had a bit of experience."

"Anybody in my position has had some experience," he replied. "That doesn't mean a whole lot necessarily. It's just that sometimes we have experiences in life that we wish we didn't."

"Yeah, I've had a few of those already," she admitted. "This will just be another to add to the list, I suppose."

"That's another reason to solve the problem, and, if it turns out to be not connected, even better."

"I still can't imagine anybody caring about that video,"

she muttered.

"Someone is worried about what could have been captured on that video. Something was going on in that vicinity." He asked, "What if somebody was hired to hang around the ER, until he got news about Mason's condition?"

"But how would they even get that? It's not as if we would have told some random strangers."

"Maybe they wouldn't need to be told. Anybody in that waiting room would easily have seen Tesla's reaction and even overhead conversations."

She winced, as she thought about it and nodded. "That's very true, and it wouldn't have taken much detective work to realize Mason was still alive."

"Exactly, and the fact that he is still alive is an issue somebody may care about. They would know it, one way or another."

"People suck," she announced.

He laughed. "I won't argue with you on that because I happen to agree. They definitely suck." He nodded, a smile on his face. "Still, that doesn't change the fact that, right now, Mason is under guard, and you can't be left alone, not until we solve the case of this hit-and-run."

"It was nothing," she murmured. He just nodded and didn't say anything. "It would sure be nice if you believed me."

"I won't believe anything until I have proof," he replied coolly, lifting his head from the laptop he was working on.

"Is that what you've been doing here?"

"It sure is," he said, with a smile. "You were sleeping, so what would I do? Nothing?"

She frowned and then shrugged. "I wasn't thinking you would be doing anything," she murmured. "I was hoping this was just an accident and it would all go away."

"What do you think now?"

"I still think that," she replied, wincing at his tone.

"You think or you hope?"

"Hope," she admitted, "and, until I know otherwise, I'll stay with that theory."

"You do that," he said, "and, until I know otherwise, I'll be staying with my supposition."

"Which is?"

"That you're in danger, so I won't be letting you out of my sight."

CHAPTER 7

AMBER SETTLED DOWN after that last minor dispute about who would stay and who would be allowed to go back to work, unclear at this point. She hadn't thought through the consequences of going back to work, and Jasper knew for a fact that no way she was capable for a few days. She'd taken a hard hit, and her body would be very sore and stiff for several days.

At the very least, she needed to spend the next two days and the weekend looking after herself. Jasper would arrange somebody else to come and relieve him, so he could carry on the battle he was waging to figure all this out.

He picked up the phone, while she was sipping tea, and called the hospital. As soon as he got through, he asked for an update on Mason's condition. With that relayed to him, he hung up and smiled with satisfaction. "Mason is still holding his own."

"I wouldn't be at all surprised if he comes out of this in great condition," she shared. When Jasper frowned at her, she shrugged. "He's young. He's strong. He has everything to live for."

He contemplated that for a long moment and agreed with her on every point. "That he does."

"I still don't understand why you're so worked up about it though," she began. "I get that you are part of the investigation team, but—"

"No *but* about it. He's also family."

She stared at him skeptically. "Seriously?"

He nodded. "Why does that surprise you?"

"I don't know. I guess Telsa mentioned that you are family, but I put it down to … I don't know, in my line of work, lots of people claim family relationships that turn out to be more sentimental than blood based. I guess I hadn't thought it through, and, if you did tell me, I don't remember," she admitted, with a headshake. "Some days at work are just like that."

"Some days are like that. Plus things don't always need to be separated by work."

"No, that's true too," she admitted, with half a smile. "It always seems so much is going on in life that it's hard to keep track of people's relationships."

He nodded and didn't say anything more and kept clicking away on the keyboard.

"How come you didn't phone Tesla?"

"I did earlier, but it went to voice mail. I don't want to wake her if she's sleeping." Almost as if on cue, his phone rang. He smiled as he looked at the number and said in a proud tone, "That's her now. Hey, Tesla. How are you doing, sweetie?"

"I'm doing better," she replied, her voice low and dragging. "Exhausted, but Mason is holding on, so I can't ask for anything more than that, right?"

"Sure, you can," he replied. "You can ask for the world, and you know that I'll do everything I can to give it to you. And, in this case, we've also got the whole base wanting to help."

He heard the smile in her voice when she said, "You've always been like that, haven't you?"

"If there's anything I could have done to prevent this, I would have done it. However, for the moment, we're stuck in whatever nightmare this is."

"And that's why I'm calling," she stated. "Is there any update? Do you have any news?"

"No, I don't, and now we have a different development we're sorting out." Then he quickly explained about Amber's hit-and-run.

"Oh my God," Tesla cried out. "Is she okay?"

"She is. In fact, I'm at her apartment, keeping an eye on her, and she is glaring at me right now because she doesn't want to believe any of this is connected or that she is in any trouble."

Tesla went quiet for a moment. "But how could we *not* think it's connected?" she asked in a businesslike tone. "She was there when Mason came in and took such good care of me and was back and forth, checking up on me and Mason. … It has to be connected."

"Exactly. So, you stay put. If you need anything, let me know, and I'll run by the house and get it for you—unless you want to go get it yourself."

"One thing I was wondering about," she said, "is my father is taking care of Sebastian. They might need some support, and I'm not sure they can get through this without me."

"Well, they will," he said, "and eventually we can bring Sebastian in to see you and his dad, but I think it's better if we wait a little bit longer, just from a security point of view. Also, it would probably be best if we waited, you know, with

Mason in his condition. ... Let's have him wake up first before Sebastian sees his dad."

"Oh, absolutely," she said quietly, "I would love to see him though."

"Do you want to visit Sebastian and leave Mason?"

"Leave Mason? No," she snapped. "That's not an option."

"Then the status quo holds," he confirmed. "I can go visit with him, if you want, and maybe give your dad an update."

"Yes, please do. And if you would do that maybe in person ..." She let it trail off because she knew that was asking a lot of him.

"Yeah, I'm working on that. I've spoken to them a couple times already."

"Oh good," she said. "I never know what everybody else is doing. My world is narrowed down to Mason's recovery, and that's it."

"That is your world right now," Jasper agreed. "Mason's recovery is everything. So just hold tight, and let's keep everything focused, so we don't have anything go haywire at this point. I will let you know if anything develops. I also still need that list of suspects from you."

"I've thought about it over and over," she explained, "and I'm not at all sure anybody would know anything. ... You would have to talk to his team."

"I've got members of the investigative team on base talking with his team right now, seeing if anything new came up, but we have nothing for now."

"Check his emails," she suggested suddenly.

"I'll check on it," Jasper said because something rang true. "Did he tell you anything about a problem while he was up north?"

"There were lots of problems while he was up north," she stated. "He went up there himself because some of the issues just needed an extra set of eyes and a fresh perspective. He couldn't do that while he was down here. He was there for a few weeks, but I know he figured that everything was solved. He was sad too because he knew a bunch of the people involved."

"It's always sad when we know the people involved," Jasper concurred.

"You know about that too, don't you?" she asked, with a groan. "Sometimes, the world, well, … you know, people suck." Having just heard that from Amber, his gaze flicked over in her direction to see her smiling.

"That is quite right. Amber just mentioned something very similar," he shared, with a gentle chuckle. "All you need to focus on right now is Mason and you and that baby," Jasper reiterated. "I'll handle the rest. Now, go take a nap."

"Yes, sir," Tesla replied, and then she laughed. "I am tired, so maybe that is what I need. I might need some clothes at some point too."

"Tell me what you need," he said. "I told you that I'll get it."

"I'll text you a list, after my nap." And, with that, she was gone.

He looked over at Amber. "Tesla appears to be holding up okay."

"She's good people," she noted, "and she's been to hell and back already."

"Isn't that the truth, but she is very good at sorting through the priorities. I've known her through thick and thin. Our families were estranged for a while, but we kept in touch. When she married Mason, we got a whole lot closer."

"Sounds like you and Mason had more in common than you had with your family."

"Yeah, well, that is an understatement. It's one of the reasons that I was coming here to work with Mason. I was about to walk away from the work completely," he admitted, shaking his head. "I was sick to the soul, but they convinced me to go back, which is why I was just starting again at this location."

"I'm sorry. I can't imagine the work you do."

"It can be stressful," he said, keeping his gaze steady. "It can be debilitating mentally and emotionally. Then, when you discover good friends are involved in the crimes you've been investigating," he shared, his lips twitching, "it can be beyond debilitating."

"That sounds awful," Amber muttered, with a sad smile. "The worst thing I ever had along that line, and it certainly hurt, … but I came into the ER, started my shift, and an ambulance rolled in with my best friend." She looked directly at him.

As her head twisted away, he saw the glint of tears. "What happened?"

"We did everything we could, and we couldn't save her," she whispered. "There's nothing, *nothing* like finding out somebody you cared about, somebody you deal with, … day in, day out, is …"

"Was it an accident?"

She looked over at him and shook her head. "She committed suicide, and everybody at the ER knew her. We were absolutely horrified, and the fact that we couldn't do anything for her just made it that much worse."

He winced. "Of course then I would guess the next level

is wondering how it got to that point, and why you couldn't have saved her before it even came to being in the ER."

She nodded. "That's the next thing that happened. You question how is it that you didn't know she was so troubled, how is it that you didn't know that she needed you, if you were such good friends." She took a moment to hold back the tears. "The guilt is crippling, and yet that's not why the person does it, of course. It's not why they're in the situation, but it doesn't help you to stop feeling as if you could have and should have done more," she murmured.

"Yes," he noted in a calm tone. "In my situation, I was on a case, looking for somebody running a lot of drugs through the military." He shook his head, and, when she gasped in shock, he nodded. "Whenever you get people together, people have a way of being people, no matter where they end up."

"So, what happened?"

"It just got out of control and wasn't what I thought. I got chumped in a big way, but it doesn't matter. It's just that, after something like that, I don't even want to deal with people anymore."

"Sounds horrible," she muttered, not fully understanding, but, since he was skirting around the edges, she knew there must have been a lot more to it.

"What a mess," he said, "but that's life."

She nodded. "I can't say I've been through anything quite like that."

"It doesn't matter," he replied, with a wave of his hand. "It's not a contest. It's just one of those things that you realize is part of it all. We all have histories. We all have relationships that go bad. We all have childhoods that had trauma. We all have these things that we should deal with but haven't yet, and they come back and hit you in the face, time and time again. You hope that you can deal with them. You hope that you can get out of them, but there's no guarantee, even if you do, that life will be any better."

"That's a pessimistic view."

"Not at all," he argued, shaking his head. As he opened his mouth to speak again, the doorbell rang.

She jolted, looking over at him.

"Are you expecting anybody?" he asked.

She shook her head. "No. Not only that, … I never get people here. I deliberately keep this address private."

He frowned. "No deliveries? Particularly after COVID and all? … So many people went for online ordering."

"I haven't ordered anything in a very long time," she shared.

He nodded. "Stay there."

"As if I'll move much anyway," she muttered, as he got up. She watched as he silently moved to the front door. She had no little window in the door or even a peephole to look out. The only way to look outside and see who was at her door was through the nearby window.

JASPER SHIFTED THE curtains slightly, just in time to see a vehicle pulling away. Frowning, he opened the curtain wider to take a better look to see if somebody was still at the door. Seeing nothing, he stepped forward and opened the door just a hair and looked around. Still nothing he could see. As he pulled open the door wider, he found a piece of paper on the ground.

He picked it up, took one look, and read the message.

His jaw firmed up, as he stared down at the warning message, before he stepped out into the hallway and looked around.

Amber shrunk into the couch, as he walked back into the living room and handed her the note. "Just in case you have any more doubts," he stated.

She looked at the warning note and read it out loud. "*Keep your nose out of other people's business, bitch.*"

"Says something, *huh*?"

"And yet," she replied, staring at it in shock, "it still doesn't confirm anything."

"No, it doesn't confirm anything," he agreed calmly, "but it doesn't exactly give us clarity either."

She stared at him and shrugged. "Maybe my instincts picked up on how they were up to something, and now they want to ensure I don't say anything," she suggested, raising both hands. "The more disconcerting thought for me is how did they know where I live?"

"Knowing where you live could simply involve following us, hacking into computer systems, or just asking people where you work," he said. "It isn't all that hard, if you have any skills, and, in this case, we have people with skills."

She cried out in exasperation, "But sniper skills are a long way from hunting down people, by hacking and finding addresses."

He gave her a wry look. "They have your name, and they know what vehicle you drive, and the DMV would most likely give them an address."

She swallowed. "But—"

He shook his head. "No buts," he said, raising his voice. "This is no longer an accident. You've already been attacked, now threatened, and you need to accept that. Obviously we have a bigger problem than we were hoping, and, while it would be nice to think it's not connected to the shooting of Mason, I have to assume that it is."

She sat here and glared at him, clearly disgruntled.

His lips quirked at the pouty little child in front of him. "I get it," he said, with a chuckle. "You don't want it to be connected. You don't want anything to do with any of this."

"No, I don't," she exclaimed, "and I thought I was in the clear."

"I know you did, but, once you got run over, all bets were off." When she winced at that, he nodded. "No other way to put it," he declared. "Obviously somebody was out to get you, and they made their first attempt with a car, and now they know where you live."

Her face paled at that, and she looked around the room. "I must admit how that part concerns me. I'm nobody, but they have my address. That scares me."

"It should," he agreed, "because we don't want anybody coming back here, thinking that you live alone."

"Would they have stayed around?"

"Maybe not with me here, but thinking you have a boyfriend still doesn't fully protect you. … I can't be here all the time, and they may very well have somebody outside, who saw me pick up the note. You don't know who these people are or what they're up to."

"I don't want to either," she declared, glaring at him.

He loved the fact that she had shifted from angry to scared and was back to angry again. "Keep up the anger," he stated. "It's a whole lot better than the fear of being a victim."

"Yet, that's what I am, isn't it?" she asked, staring at him, her eyes widening at the thought.

"No, I won't say that," he clarified. "It's not healthy to be a victim, so let's not go that route. You need to think this through for now. Stay angry, stay in control, and realize that somebody is pushing your buttons and is scaring you into doing something. The trouble is, that note doesn't tell us what they want you to do."

"He wants my *nose out* apparently," she stated, with a snort. "Like what the hell do they think I even did?"

"I suspect they know you took that video. They just don't know what you captured on that video. And they are obviously worried about something captured on film."

"But people take videos all the time," she said impatiently. "If they didn't want people to know what they were up to, they shouldn't have been talking in that location." He shot her a sideways glance, and she flushed. "Fine, all right, so it wasn't the smartest idea, and I get it. At the same time, I don't want it thrown in my face until I'm old and gray."

"Wasn't planning on it," he replied cheerfully. "I just want to know what this is about. If it has nothing to do with the assassination attempt on Mason, then the last thing I want to do is waste time investigating the wrong matter."

"Then go investigate Mason," she exclaimed, glaring at him. "I'm not here to take you away from that."

"You aren't making me do anything," he admitted, staring at her. "As a matter of fact, if you had your druthers, you would have forced me out of here a long time ago."

She flushed. "I wouldn't be that rude," she said stiffly.

He burst into laughter. "Oh, you would so."

She flushed a brighter red and then came back with another retort. "Honestly, I just want this all to go away."

"Okay, so if you were alone, and you had answered that doorbell, particularly if you'd answered it right away," he began, "what would your reaction have been?" She stared at him, nonplussed. He nodded. "Your reaction would be to turn around and phone somebody. So now you've got somebody here, who'll be looking for a bigger explanation as to what's going on."

"Maybe I wouldn't have called anybody," she replied. "Maybe I would have just kept it to myself. How can you be sure of that?"

"It crossed my mind, but then, when your dead body shows up in a few days in some alleyway, or if somebody comes to check on why you didn't show up at work, and they find you dead on your couch, is that any better?" He watched as the color drained rapidly from her face.

"Exactly," he stated. "I'm not trying to scare you, but to warn you. Also I'm not here to create a villain where there isn't one or to make a bigger deal out of this than it already is. That is not my intention either. We have more than enough problems without creating something out of nothing," he declared, shaking his head, "but regardless if this is related to Mason or not, it's obviously a problem for you, and one we have to solve before you are free to move around again."

He sighed. "In fact, as it is right now, you're also incapable of moving around because of that hit-and-run. Maybe that was something they wanted too. Maybe they wanted you injured, incapacitated, maybe at home instead of the hospital, so they could come here and get the information they wanted from you, or maybe they were looking for that video."

She stared at him. "Are you talking from experience?"

"Yes. However, I don't know what their threat entails, what they plan to do next," he conceded, "but that is a threat against you. And that's just making me incredibly frustrated. Have you reviewed the tape further? Maybe you missed something earlier?"

She sighed. "I can look at it again, but I really don't see what is so all important about this one off-the-cuff video." With a growl, she reached for her cup of tea, stared down at the empty cup, then slammed it on the coffee table, perhaps a little too hard.

He nodded because he understood what that was about. "I know exactly how you feel," he muttered, and then he laughed. "But I can still get a cup of tea for you."

"No, … forget it, and, if you weren't here, I would probably go for something a hell of a lot stronger." He stared at her with interest, and she shrugged. "Just kidding, but maybe coffee would be better."

"Good," he said, with a nod. "I can do coffee, and, if you're fussy about the way you like it, you can just sit there and tell me how you want it."

"I'm not fussy," she replied. "Right now I'm just sad. I hadn't expected this turn of events."

"No, I'm sure you didn't," he agreed. "I don't think any of us did, but it's one thing to get run down and have it be an accident. It's an entirely different thing to now have somebody come to your house and threaten you with violence if you don't keep your mouth shut."

"Yet they didn't say what they would do," she pointed out, "so it's hardly a threat of violence."

He sat down hard on the couch beside her, jostling her leg. When she winced, he reached out, patting her hand. "Sorry, I didn't mean to hurt you."

"No, you didn't want to hurt me, but you do want to shake some sense into me."

He opened his eyes wide and then nodded. "I would like to do that, and it would be a hell of a lot easier if you would listen. This note probably came from the same people who ran you down. Since that wasn't enough, prompting this threatening note, do you think the next thing they have planned for you is nonviolent? I suspect it will be more violent than the hit-and-run."

"I'm listening," she stated, "but there's a limit to what I can do. Obviously right now I'm injured, and I'm not going anywhere."

"That's fine. ... I get it, but neither one of us can stay here indefinitely, and if this isn't connected to Mason, ... it's still something worrisome."

"Either way, something is simmering under the surface," she agreed.

"True, and we still have to solve it, if you plan to have a life again."

She winced. "So, will we wait to solve it?" She was exasperated and totally exhausted too by the looks of it. "This is your investigation, isn't it?"

"Yes, it's my investigation," he confirmed, looking at her, "but I have to delve into your background a whole lot deeper, and I'm pretty sure that's not something you want." She stared at him, and he watched as the last of the color drained away. He didn't think her face could get any paler. He nodded when he saw the shocked look on her face.

"Why is that?" she asked.

"Because, if this is something I'm investigating, then I have to know absolutely everything about why it's happening. So, I'll have to narrow down the facts and see what I can find for other reasons—not Mason-related—that you may not realize where somebody would hurt you, would retaliate."

"Nobody'll hurt me," she said stiffly.

He frowned. "You keep saying things like that, and yet—"

"Yet what?" she asked.

"Yet I don't believe you. It seems to me that we have a bigger mystery here than maybe you've let on."

"I don't have any secrets, if that's what you mean. I don't have any murdered family members who have come back to haunt me. I don't have any of that stuff," she said, her voice rising an octave higher. "I've been a nurse, working at this hospital for a very long time, and I'm hardly someone who anybody gives a crap about."

"And yet somebody does give a crap about something here," Jasper declared, as he tossed the note back down on the coffee table in front of her. "Somebody cares a hell of a lot, and forgetting about that fact," he snapped, taking a moment, while she waited and seemed to be listening, "*forgetting* will get you killed."

TESLA SHIFTED IN her seat, reminded that the cramping was horrific today. She'd tried to hide it from anybody around her because she didn't want to listen to any more comments about what she should and should not do, especially the people who told her to go home. As for the baby, well, … the baby was definitely not impressed today.

Whether the hospital food, the stress, or the sleeplessness, Tesla didn't know, but she was getting a good workout from the inside out, and it was a little bit too much today.

She got up and slowly paced the small hospital room.

Her world had shrunk down to just this, to her beloved husband, waiting for him to wake up, waiting for him to show signs of anything. Doctors and nurses came and went, muttered, and nodded, gave her half smiles, then quickly disappeared, knowing that she would ask questions. So far, it appeared that nobody had any answers. The hospital, the baby, and hope were the only constants in this equation for the last few days, and that was that.

That was the worst part—the waiting, the not knowing what was going on, not understanding how something like this could continue to be a mystery in this world. Surely they could do more for her husband than to keep him in this coma.

And they used all kinds of medical words that Tesla had been busy looking up, but nothing that told her anything, as if they didn't know themselves. Most of them basically just told her *too early to say anything definitive, to give him time, that he was working on his healing, he was alive, and his body was working on coming back to her.* She wanted to believe them; she had to because the other option was out of the question.

When a knock came on the door to Mason's hospital room, she turned to see it burst open, and her little boy raced to her. He cried out, "Mommy," and threw himself into her arms. She held him tightly against her and just rocked him on the edge of the cot. It was so damn good to see him, but, at the same time, it was also damn scary to even begin to think that he was here. He was only three years old, and so much of this was scary for him.

Was it even safe for Sebastian to be here?

Well, that was a question she would love to have an answer for, and quick. She didn't know anything about it. She looked over to see Markus standing there, his arms crossed, as Sebastian babbled away.

"Uncle Markus brought me. He said Grandad needed a break." Sebastian gave her a big, fat grin.

"Oh, did he now?" Tesla asked.

Sebastian nodded.

"I can't imagine why," Tesla said in a dry tone.

Sebastian looked over and said in a coo, "Daddy is sleeping?" Such a wealth of disappointment filled his tone that it made her smile.

"Yes, honey. Daddy got hurt, so now he's sleeping, … so he can heal."

"Good," he said, "I want him to come play ball with me."

"When he feels better and when he's back home again, then we'll line that up," she said, chuckling. She let Sebastian ramble on, answering his questions, just enjoying holding the squirmy little three-year-old whom she loved with all her heart.

When she looked up at Markus, his gaze narrowed on her face. She glared at him. "I'm fine." He just raised an eyebrow and didn't say a word, as she groaned. "So, today might not be the greatest day as a pregnant woman," she admitted, with a shrug, as she shifted Sebastian around.

"*Huh.*"

"Yeah, and *that* … doesn't mean anything." He didn't respond, which was in some ways even worse. "Honest, Markus, I'm fine."

"I'm glad to hear that," he said quietly, "because you know, when Mason gets out of this, if anything happened to you in the meantime, … he'll have every one of our heads."

She winced and then chuckled. "That is something to

keep you guys in line at least."

"It'll keep us in line," he said, with a warning look in her direction, "by keeping you in line."

She didn't like that at all, but she understood it. "I'm fine. Baby's just extra-active today."

At that, Sebastian patted her belly several times and said, "When is baby coming?" He cried out loud enough for people to hear him loud and clear, making her blush. "I want baby."

"Baby's coming soon enough," she said. "Baby's not fully cooked yet."

Sebastian looked at her and then giggled. "Like cookies?"

"Something like that," she said, with half a laugh. The absolute innocence in his face and his tone of voice always put a smile on hers. She looked over at Markus and whispered, "Thank you."

He nodded. "We can't stay too long. After this, we're going bowling."

"Bowling?" she repeated.

At that, Sebastian went off in squeals of delight, hearing the word from her. "They're really big balls," he said excitedly. "Uncle Markus has to take them off the rack, but I'm really good at rolling them down the runway."

She blinked at the thought, her mind kicking in at seeing her little toddler, with Markus standing behind him, helping him push. She slid a glance over at Markus, who had a big grin on his face. "What about Bree?" she asked of his wife.

"She's thrilled. If you ask me, she would keep this guy forever."

"Well, she can't have him," Tesla declared and then chuckled. "However, I really do appreciate that everybody is pitching in to keep him company."

"Of course they're pitching in," he said, with a grin. "You know we all love this guy," Markus said, as he pointed to the bed where Mason was crashed. "He just needs to wake up."

"He does, indeed," she said, glaring over at the bed where her husband was snuggled in. "The sooner, the better."

He laughed. "You know him. He's always got to do a job the right way," he said. "He'll come out when he's darn good and ready and not before."

She laughed. "Isn't that the truth," she murmured affectionately.

Just then Markus turned to Sebastian and said, "Come on, buddy. Time to go push those bowling balls."

"Yeah!" He raced to the door and then stopped and ran back to Tesla and threw his arms around her and gave her a big, sloppy kiss. "Bye, Mommy." And, with that, he was gone.

She sighed, wondering where the world just went, as it seemed to have come and gone in her life with the aplomb of a very confident and happy little boy. One thing she had done well in this world was her little guy. Sebastian was her one true success in this world. He was a very well-adjusted and happy little boy, and, although she didn't want to think of a life without his daddy, she knew that they would get through it one way or another, if they had to.

She was so damn grateful that she had Sebastian right now, a light in her life. Given the circumstances, she was also damn grateful for all his well-respected uncles because they made her bedside vigil, watching over Mason, a hell of a lot easier right now.

With that thought, she shifted back onto the cot, closed her eyes, and curled up for yet another nap.

CHAPTER 8

L ATER THAT NIGHT, as Amber tried desperately to fall asleep, her mind swirled endlessly from one danger to another that her foolish actions may have gotten her into. She didn't have any history that she could think of that would lead to this current threat. However, it made more sense that her hit-and-run was connected to Mason's shooting, since she had been at the hospital and had foolishly taken that video. She had reviewed the video multiple times now. Nothing stood out to her. And, if this violence directed at her was connected to that video, how could she possibly let these strangers know that she wasn't a threat, when in their minds she was probably too big of a threat already. Her thoughts kept running wild.

The threatening note didn't bother her so much as the fact that it could just be a prelude to something much worse, and that was a concern and not anything she wanted to consider. She was a sitting duck here, being injured as she was. Since Jasper had opened the door to find the note, if they had been watching and recognized him, did they know what was going on? It just seemed as if so much could be involved in the way of ugly options, and she had no idea how to even begin to free herself from this mess.

One thing she knew was that she was fighting Jasper tooth and nail. God only knows why she was giving Jasper such grief. She appreciated the fact that she wasn't here alone and couldn't imagine being all alone right now, wondering and worrying whether these guys would come back. In her mind, they would definitely come back. She had hoped that maybe seeing Jasper here would have been a deterrent, but it might just as easily have been the opposite. They might have decided that he was a problem and needed to be taken out too.

When a light knock came on her bedroom door, she called out, "Come in."

Jasper walked in and smiled. "I didn't think you would be sleeping."

"I wish I was," she murmured, as she shifted in bed, barely wincing this time.

He noticed that. "So, either the pain pills are good or you're starting to feel a little better."

"I'm tired and I'm sore, but I am feeling a little bit better," she confessed. "It's just a strange scenario right now."

"It is," he agreed, "and I want you to leave this place."

She squeaked out in shock, "My home?"

"Yes, leave your home."

She shook her head. "I don't want to run. I don't want to leave my apartment to these guys," she added in a firm tone. "I get it. It's not all that great, and I could probably find another place to live, but why should I let them force me from my home?"

"It's a lovely little place," he agreed calmly. "Yet again, if this is connected to Mason's deal—and I don't see how it can't be—they know where you live, so let's have you live somewhere else."

"But if I leave, eventually they'll find me again," she stated, struggling to keep the bitterness from her tone. "All they have to do is follow me from work. Apparently these guys are pros. I don't quite understand how I got into this mess, but I'm even more confused as to how to get out of it."

"Getting out of it isn't easy," Jasper shared, with a nod. "We'll have to solve the Mason problem in order to have that happen."

"Good, feel free."

"I would, except that now you've been threatened and quite likely because of me, so I can't go very far."

She glared at him. "I'm not holding you responsible. Taking that video was my fault and my fault only."

"If I hadn't asked you to keep an eye out, I doubt that you would be in this situation."

She didn't know what to say to that because it may be true, except for the fact that she often kept an eye out on people. Therefore, maybe it wouldn't have made any difference at all. She knew it would be hard to convince Jasper of that. "I don't want you feeling guilty," she said, with a groan. "I just want all of this to go away."

"Yeah, well, denial has never worked for me, and I can see that you might want to try it, but I can tell you right now that it'll get worse before it gets better."

She winced. "You could just lie for a change."

He chuckled. "No, that won't help anybody."

"Maybe not, but it would make me feel better," she complained, gritting her teeth.

"It might make you feel better, but it'll be temporary. Let's get you someplace where they don't know where you're staying, and then we have a chance to get them off your tail."

"Where would you like me to go?"

He hesitated, then said, "I was thinking of my place."

Her eyebrows shot up, and she stared at him. "Isn't that taking the caretaking one step too far?"

"Not if it keeps you alive," he replied easily. "I don't know who they are or when they'll come back," he said, pointing to the door, "but I do believe that they will come back."

"But that would imply that I was a threat—well, I guess they see me that way, what with the note."

He nodded. "Or it implies that they're just tying up loose threads," he suggested, keeping his tone casual. "You've got to understand that, with a sniper shooting like that—an assassination attempt in my mind—it'll be the end of them. They will never see daylight again for what they did to Mason on base, and that's if they physically survive. So these guys won't hesitate to wipe out any evidence of their crime, whether eyewitnesses or hard data."

She winced. "Even with the base investigation ongoing, is it bad to hope that, with Mason having as many supporters as he has, an awful lot of gun-happy people are out there to get justice?"

"It's not like that, but a lot of good, law-abiding men who have worked with Mason for a very long time will be seriously looking for these guys and won't be all that fussy about taking them in alive, should they choose to go that route."

She nodded. "Right, so these shooters are under pressure. They must know everyone is looking for them."

"That's my point," he agreed. "They are backed in a corner, and you are on their radar."

She looked around at her bedroom, realizing that one of the reasons she was so grateful he was here because her place had been … violated. No, that was the wrong word, but her apartment no longer gave her that contented feeling of coming home to her own space. "I hate the fact that this place no longer feels like it's mine. It doesn't feel like home anymore."

"That's because for you it's been a sanctuary," he explained. "A sanctuary you needed, coming home after your ER shifts. Now that your sanctuary has been disturbed, it's much harder to see this place as the same haven."

"When would you want to move?" she asked.

"How quickly can you pack?" he asked, with a note of humor.

Startled, she frowned. "Tonight?"

He gave her a quick nod. "Yeah, that's what my instincts are telling me right now." He walked over to the closet, opened it up, and pulled out a couple big carry bags, then asked her, "How about we just fill this and go? It's not as if you're sleeping anyway."

She checked his facial expression to see if he was serious, realizing he probably would never joke about something like this. She nodded and pushed back the covers and sat up. "Not exactly how I expected to spend the night, but I wasn't sleeping anyway."

"Exactly," he said encouragingly. "That's the attitude."

She rolled her eyes. "None of that cheerleader stuff now," she mumbled, as she hobbled slowly over to the dresser. She had him open one of the bags and quickly emptied the contents of her dresser, then grabbed a change of clothes to get into. Afterward she went over to the closet, where she emptied out what she thought she would need for a few days. Yet, realizing that this change of location could be longer than that, she added several more things.

As she looked back at the closet, she muttered, "I didn't realize I owned so little clothing."

"I suspect you mostly wear your uniforms, don't you?"

She nodded. "Which reminds me, I should get the clothes in the laundry hamper." And, with that thought, and a plastic bag, she gathered the clothes from the hamper and finished packing up several pairs of shoes in another plastic bag. She sighed, then stepped into the bathroom to get dressed. Afterward she looked around and frowned, followed by a laugh. "Honest to God, pretty well everything that I need is packed."

"Good," Jasper noted. "That means, if anything does happen, you won't need to hit a store very quickly."

"No, I don't think so," she muttered, still quite startled at just how quickly she'd packed up her personal life. As she moved carefully into the living room, she grabbed her electronics—her phone, the phone charger, laptop, and her e-reader that she used all the time.

Within minutes, Jasper had packed up any of the food that would spoil over the next few days in another bag and began loading everything into his truck. It was dark out, past midnight, and he gave a subtle look around. He came back for her. "Grab a coat and let's go."

She cast one long last look around the living room, then did as he said and followed him outside. "You think this is the best way?"

"Yes, I think it's the *only* way at this point."

She winced but kept on moving. As she got into the truck, the pain kicked in again, and it took her a few minutes to catch her breath.

"If you were to stay here, and they were to return ..." Jasper repeated.

She waved him off. "I got that, Mr. Reality Check …"

That struck home, and he nodded, about to say something.

"Don't even go there," she stated. "Even though I've been giving you a hard time, I do realize just how much I would not want to be alone in that apartment right now."

"Exactly, and this way you won't be." Jasper smiled. "I promise that you'll be safe at my place."

"Yeah, do you live in Fort Knox or what?"

He chuckled. "Not quite, but not far off."

She frowned at him with interest, as he drove through the city and off the base. "Just even getting off base is a nice thing, isn't it?"

"Personally I prefer to live off base myself," he shared. "It helps me to detach from work. And not having a partner isn't a requirement for living on base."

"I wanted to ask about that," Amber added, "but I figured that you must have a very understanding partner, if she was okay with my moving in."

He chuckled. "No. No partner to run this by."

She felt a quiet sense of satisfaction at the thought, even though she also felt stupid. Absolutely nothing was personal about what he was doing. This was all about guilt, pure and simple. At that, she frowned. "You don't need to do this out of guilt, you know?"

"I'm not doing it out of guilt, but I could never live with myself if I found out you had gotten hurt any worse than you already are," he replied.

She winced but nodded.

A few minutes later, he pulled up in front of a small house and said, "Welcome home."

She looked at it with interest. "Can't say it looks like

Fort Knox," she teased cheerfully.

"Ah, wait until you get inside."

Surprised, she watched as he parked inside a garage, then he came around, opened the passenger side, and helped her out. He released an alarm and opened the door and got her inside to the couch. He quickly unloaded all the bags at once. She watched in amazement as he carried everything inside.

"I had a dog, but my old guy finally passed away," he stated, "so, at the moment, I don't have any pets."

"I'm sorry," she said. "Our furry friends are hard to let go of."

"He was seventeen, with a long life well lived, but it became time to let him go," he shared. "Yeah, hard to do."

She liked him even more in that moment. Anybody who could grieve over a pet couldn't be all bad. Although, from a personal safety perspective, if it weren't for Tesla confirming that this guy was okay, Amber would never have been in this situation. If any other woman had told her that she would be doing this, staying at a stranger's house, Amber would have called her out as being stupid because … Amber *didn't* know this guy. Yet in many ways she did know Jasper, and, in circumstances like this, she couldn't be choosy about her guardian angel.

And she had been damn lucky to have one, to have *this* one.

JASPER HOPED THAT, with the mental fugue Amber was in, she didn't realize somebody had been sitting outside her apartment or that they had been followed. He'd done several maneuvers to ditch their tail, and, as far as he was concerned, it had worked. Now in his house, he wanted her upstairs under the covers, where she could get some rest. Not that it would be all that easy to fall asleep, but, so far, she hadn't seemed to recognize the legitimate danger she was in.

As he took her on a quick tour of the first floor, he asked her if she could handle taking the stairs. She nodded absentmindedly, as she looked around, and he saw the interest clearly in her gaze. He had gotten that response from women before, when he had brought them here. He had spent a lot of time working on this house and had invested a lot of himself in its renovations. He had inherited the old family home from his parents. He had finished a lot of the work that his father had started, continuing it himself, keeping it at the same level and quality that he knew his father would appreciate. Working on it with memories in mind had proven to be cathartic and something he always enjoyed.

Not that everything had been easy to do because time changed everything, but he was working on making it a beautiful home. He figured that Amber would be too tired to notice, but she was seemingly not so tired that several of the architectural aspects made her stop in place and stare.

He grabbed her possessions and nudged her toward the curved open staircase, made with solid oak. "Come on. Let's get you to bed."

"This is truly a beautiful home," she whispered.

"My family home," he shared, "and I've put a lot of time and effort into making it work for us."

"Us?"

He nodded. "Honoring my parents' memories and doing all the renovations."

She nodded. "How absolutely blessed you are to have this."

He hadn't considered that, but he truly was blessed in many ways. He nodded at the open doorway they now stood before. "Come on. You're exhausted. Let's get you to bed." He followed her inside, setting her bags on the floor nearby.

"I am tired," she admitted, "but I'm also waiting for you to tell me the truth."

He stilled, then turned to look at her. "What do you mean?"

"No way something more major isn't wrong here," she declared, noting his hesitation. "I'll do much better with the truth, so let's have it, please."

He nodded. "Okay, but no freaking out then."

She winced. "Now that's guaranteed to keep me calm."

He chuckled. "I saw somebody staring at your apartment, while we were there," he said, "and I didn't like knowing someone was keeping an eye on it."

She stopped. "Somebody was sitting outside, watching my apartment?"

He nodded.

"And it wouldn't have been like, I don't know, security or something?" she asked, with an eyebrow raised.

"In this case, no. It wasn't security, at least not security that anybody told me about," he noted, taking a moment, "and they would have."

"So, you're saying that the bad guys were keeping track of me?"

"That is my assumption, … yes," he murmured, "but I don't know for sure."

She didn't know what to say to that and wore a half-stunned look on her face. She nodded. "Well, I appreciate your telling me the truth."

"One more thing," he added, then took a deep breath. "We were also tailed."

She stilled in the act of pulling back the bedcovers, then straightened and turned to look at him. "To here?" she asked, fear rising in her tone.

"Not the whole way but, yes, that would have been their plan. However, I got rid of them."

She blinked at that and nodded. "Of course you did." Looking around, she took a slow, hesitant breath. "So, you're sure we're safe?"

"We're safe here. I have lots of security outside, and it's not exactly an easy place to get to."

"I don't remember a whole lot about the trip to tell you the truth. A gate, that's about all I remember from outside."

"We'll talk about it more when you get up," he said, "but right now you need sleep."

"You're right. I definitely do," she mumbled, "and I need answers, but apparently I won't get them all, and certainly not yet."

He chuckled. "No, but we'll talk in the morning." He grabbed her toiletry bag and went into the ensuite bathroom and set it on the counter for her. "I've got towels here, if you want them."

"I'll try for a shower in the morning, but right now I'm just too tired to do anything."

"As long as you get some sleep."

"I was planning on sleeping," she stated, "until you told me about the man."

He winced and nodded. "That's why I didn't want to tell you, but you didn't want me to hold anything back."

"No, I didn't," she agreed, "and sometimes it would be

nice if I could ignore this issue, but I'm still better off knowing. Anyway, let me grab some sleep, and we'll talk in a bit."

And, with that, she headed into the bathroom. He turned and walked out of the bedroom, then headed to his bedroom. There he brought up the security cameras on the streets and around the property, then set up the alarms.

Maybe it was the work he did, or maybe his father being in the security business, but Jasper never could let go of the idea that the world was a dangerous place and that you're much better off if you're protected. However, he could never assume that security would give you everything you thought you needed because it never would and never could.

It just wasn't geared for that, but, on the other hand, it should give her a whole lot more confidence than she'd experienced so far. At least that would be his assumption, and he would see, come morning, if there had been any disturbances. Yet, right now, he needed to grab some sleep himself.

As he headed into his bathroom, he quickly had a shower, and checking the security feed once more and seeing nothing, he went to crash. Four hours later, he rose and checked on the system again. With no breaches noted, he headed back to bed and got another good four hours before he woke up. He lay in bed for a long moment, checking out his senses to see if anything caused a panic or even a low-grade anxiety, but internally everything felt fine. He got up and once again checked all the security feeds but found nothing amiss.

With relief, he quickly dressed and headed downstairs to put on coffee. Once the pot was made, he grabbed a cup. With the security app now up on his phone, so he could check it on a regular basis, he walked back upstairs and knocked on her door.

"I'm awake," she murmured.

He opened the door, stepped inside, and her face lit up when she saw the coffee. "Wow, delivery too?"

"The problem is, with you upstairs, coming downstairs will be that much harder on you."

She nodded. "Yeah, hard to get up the stairs last night."

"If I hadn't been carrying the luggage, I could have picked you up and brought you upstairs myself," he noted. "Sorry, I should have thought of that."

She waved her hand. "I don't do the whole invalid thing very well."

He chuckled. "That's good to know, and I guess that means you don't want coffee then, *huh*?"

"Take it away and you die," she teased, then laughed.

Smiling, he brought it over and set it down on the bedside table next to her. When his phone rang, he looked down to the Caller ID. "Markus, what's up?"

"Are you all right?" he asked, a stressed-out tone to his voice. "Have you heard from Amber?"

"I took her to my house last night, when I realized somebody was watching her place."

"Yeah? Well, somebody threw Molotov cocktails through two windows of her apartment," he snapped. "Everything inside has been destroyed. The fire department got it contained before it affected any of the other apartments, probably because she was in the corner."

CHAPTER 9

AMBER OVERHEARD THE conversation and cried out, now sitting up in the bed, staring at Jasper.

"When did it happen?" Jasper asked, wanting to calm her down, but that would not be an easy thing. She was already up and pacing around the bedroom, but he could see the pain with her every step. He pulled her into his arms and just held her, rocking her back and forth, while she sobbed silently against his chest.

"About two o'clock this morning," Markus replied. "I'm on the scene right now. Did she have any pets or anything?"

"No pets, thank God, and I brought her here just after midnight, I would say probably one-thirty a.m. or so. I'll have to check the security cameras to see what time we pulled in." He hesitated, then added, "I will tell you that we were followed too."

Markus sighed, as he digested that information. "She's definitely on somebody's shit list."

"Yeah, she definitely is," Jasper confirmed. "You may recall that my place is pretty heavily secured, so it seemed like the thing to do, once I realized she was under surveillance."

"I remember Mason saying something about Tesla's

family being heavy into security."

"Yeah, especially in this business. I own my family home, and … it's pretty-well secured."

He released her, and she sank back onto the bed, still digesting the reality that her little apartment had been destroyed. Then she had to remind herself that she could have been gone with it, if it weren't for Jasper right now, who had dragged her out of bed just after midnight, telling her that he wasn't happy and wanted to move them. She didn't know whether instincts or something more had led to this, but, damn, she owed him more than ever now.

She didn't have a problem being grateful for somebody else's actions, but she still was struggling with the loss of her place, with the intrusion, with the freedom it once represented. When he'd mentioned something about pets, it reminded her how dangerous it would be to even have a pet right now. She'd thought about getting a cat again, but not now.

No sooner had Jasper gotten off the phone from Markus, than her phone rang and his right afterward. It seemed the news had gotten out, and she spent the next twenty or thirty minutes calming down several coworkers, who had just heard the news, letting them all know that she was safe and out of her apartment at the time of the fire.

Of course several of them had theories as to what was going on, but none were based on any proof, and all she could do was smile, and say that she would take care of it. By the time she finally hung up, she was shaking. Feeling his gaze, she looked over to find Jasper studying her. "I'm fine," she said. "I've just lost my apartment and everything I left behind, but I'm okay."

"Good, I'm glad you're holding up. This isn't easy for

anybody."

"Maybe," she murmured, "but better that I wasn't at home when it happened."

"Exactly, so we can be very grateful we got out."

She half-smiled and nodded. "I'm grateful you saw the person sitting outside. Do you think they knew that we left?"

"I would think so," he replied, "unless he was falling asleep at his post."

"But if they did know, what was the point of destroying my apartment?" she asked in bewilderment. "It only makes sense if he was there to take me out."

"But it could also have been … another warning or maybe just more of a temper fit than anything else."

She shuddered. "Then somebody has got a piss-ass bad temper," she noted, "and I don't want to come up against it again."

"I don't want you to either. That's not the behavior any of us want to deal with, but it seems to be where we're at for the moment. And it just confirms that such an overt act must be connected with the sniper shooting of Mason."

She grimaced and nodded. "I get it. … I do, and I'm grateful that we're here." She gave him a nod. "I'm also very happy that I didn't see any of that happen. That would have been much harder to deal with. … Any chance of getting more coffee?"

"I'll leave you to get dressed, or do you want me to wait and help you down the stairs?"

She hesitated and shook her head. "I should be fine going down the stairs. At least let me change, then I'll give it a try."

He nodded, then disappeared.

Once he was gone, she got up, moving slowly, then got

dressed. At the top of the stairs, she took a deep breath and slowly, planting both feet on each step, she made her way down the stairs. Halfway down she heard him heading her way and looked up and smiled. "I'm doing okay, so no need to panic."

"Good. I was prepared to let you do what you could do, and, if you didn't need a hand, then I wouldn't push it."

"I appreciate that." Her next step landed a little hard, and she stopped, waiting for the jarring pain to subside, currently skittering up and down her leg.

Gently placing a hand on her shoulder, he murmured, "That's why you still need someone nearby." With that, he swung her up into his arms and carried her down the rest of the way.

She grasped his huge shoulders. "I can't imagine ever getting used to this."

"You guys carry patients all the time, don't you?" he asked, looking at her curiously.

"We have orderlies for that, and we certainly lift patients at times," she added, rolling her eyes. "I don't know so much about carrying them like this."

"Just think of this as another method."

"It's hardly the hospital-approved method," she replied with a laugh, "but I'll let you off the hook."

"Thank you, ma'am," he replied humbly.

She laughed. "That whole humble thing doesn't work for you."

He gave her a bright grin. "It always has before."

"Sure," she muttered. "I bet you were deadly in school too."

"I don't know about deadly," he clarified, with a grin, "but that was a heck of a long time ago, and I'm sure not that person anymore."

"Are any of us?" she asked, with a smile.

"Sometimes I think we are, with little bits and pieces of us that make it forward at times. We just never know."

"That's true too," she agreed. He set her down in the kitchen, and she looked around with interest. "Wow, I presume with a kitchen like this that you must cook, or is it all for show?"

He laughed. "It's not for show. I can cook and appreciate when I get the chance, which isn't all that often."

"I can imagine," she muttered, as she surveyed the room—a large country kitchen with a big island, lots of counter space, and a huge shiny stove with pots and pans hanging from above. "I always wondered what it would be like to have a kitchen like this." She stared around in fascination.

"Now you know, and, anytime you want to cook, feel free."

She laughed. "I didn't say anything about cooking very well."

"I like home-cooked food, so it doesn't matter if it's good or not. I'm okay with variety too."

She walked the last few steps to the coffeepot, and, still carrying her cup in her hand, she turned to look at him. "Do you want a cup?"

He nodded, came over with his cup, and, once they both had refills, he led her to an adjacent sunroom, which had her exclaiming all over again. "Wow, now this is what I call a sunroom."

"My mother's favorite room," he added, with an affectionate look.

"Are they both gone?"

"They are," he said, with a nod. "It's one of the reasons why Tesla and I became close. When you lose all your family, you tend to reach out, looking for others to connect with."

Amber didn't want to ask any questions, but it seemed odd that he would lose everybody.

He answered her silent question regardless. "Both gone in one car accident."

She winced. "I see it all the time at work," she murmured. "They're just deadly and so unforgiving."

"That they are," he agreed, with a nod, "and it happened so fast, with no chance to say goodbye, just no warning. From one minute to the next, game over. They were here one moment, and the next they were gone."

"It can happen like that sometimes," she muttered, "and obviously in your case that's the way it was. Yet it's not always like that. Sometimes they linger, and people have hope. Then suddenly that hope is snuffed out, and family and friends look at us like we did something to their loved one, when they were just lingering, … well past the point in time that we thought they would. It's hard for the family because it's like losing them all over again."

"And the absence of hope …" he quoted.

She smiled. "Yes, exactly."

They sat in the sunroom, with their second cups of coffee, and she studied him for a long moment. "What made you bring me here last night?"

"Instincts," he replied, with a shrug. "I didn't like that your apartment was being watched. I didn't like anything about it."

"So, you just knew?"

"Basically, yes. Then the fact that we were followed

here—or someone tried to," he noted, with an eye roll, "makes it even more suspicious." He looked down at her leg and asked, "How long are you off work?"

"At least four days, and then I have my regular four days off, so eight days total for sure. Why?"

"I just wondered how much time we have to get you healed."

"A week should be enough," she noted, looking down. "I need to start stretching and getting it a little more limber."

"Sounds painful."

"Yeah, it will be. After sleeping for a while, I hate to move, knowing everything has been stagnant for too long. However, stretching exercises are also the best way to get everything moving again."

"Only if it's healed enough."

"Only if it's healed enough," she agreed, looking down, "and maybe it has."

"Maybe it hasn't," he argued. She glared at him, and he just smiled back at her. "I know you are frustrated and in pain and aren't used to being the patient in this scenario, but you're also being stubborn."

"Yeah, and, according to you, I'm always stubborn," she murmured. Just then his phone rang again. She sighed and turned. "It'll do this all day, won't it?"

He nodded. "It will, and I suspect we'll have a lot of people over here, including the police."

"Right, and, if it was arson, they'll need to know about it too."

"They'll need to know everything, and now we'll have the fire department, the military, the local police, an insurance investigation, and God-only-knows who else in on it."

She rolled her eyes at that. "Any chance they will all talk to each other?"

"They will, but I don't know that they'll share as much as they could or would in any other circumstance," he pointed out calmly, "but we can hope."

And that's pretty much how the day went, from quiet to multiple phone calls. Almost everybody she knew connected with her to confirm that she was alive and well. She suddenly became aware that she had far more friends than she realized. Such an odd feeling to know that everybody had heard about what had happened, and, of course, they all had multiple questions as to what she was doing and why was she here with Jasper.

She didn't have an answer beyond that she needed a place to go, and this was a good choice, particularly since he was the one who had saved her life in the first place.

When her phone rang again, she was surprised to see who it was. "Tesla," she asked, clearly alarmed, "are you okay?"

"I'm fine," Tesla replied, "but I just heard about your apartment."

"Ah, yeah, that didn't exactly make my day, but I wasn't there, so that is some good news. I ended up coming to Jasper's house."

Silence came on the other end, and then Tesla teasingly said, "Wow, that's a surprise."

"And not what you're thinking," she replied, with an eye roll toward Jasper.

"I'm not thinking anything. Jasper's always been very smart, and he's very good at preempting danger."

"I don't know that he preempted anything outside of my seeing my apartment burn. I have to admit that wasn't happy news. I'm sure the landlord will be more than pissed off about the whole thing."

"Not your problem," she said. "You need to heal. It's bad enough that you were injured, without the bad guys attempting to take you out while you were already down."

"Doesn't say much for them, does it? When you think about it, that's an awful lot of nastiness to take out on somebody. I guess they really intended to take me out with the car."

"Exactly," Tesla agreed, "but, if Jasper took you to his house, you're in Fort Knox."

"He did mention something like that." Amber laughed. "I appreciate his listening to his instincts and caring enough to get me out of there."

"You're safe there," Tesla shared, "so please take off however much time you can from work and heal. I don't know what these assholes are after, but I can only assume that it's connected to Mason."

"Speaking of Mason, how is he?"

Tesla's words were caught on a sob. "He still hasn't woken up."

"He will when he's ready to," Amber reiterated. "He's got an awful lot of healing to do in there."

"Yeah, the doctor said that too," she murmured, "but it's very hard to see him like this. I need him awake, and I need him to know that I'm here and that I love him."

"Tesla," Amber whispered, "he already knows it in his heart. That is not something he needs to hear you say only while he's conscious. That's you feeling that you need to say it when you know he hears you. Yet I believe he does hear you, even while unconscious. He loves you, and he knows you know that too."

They talked a few more minutes, and then they ended the call. Amber found Jasper looking at her curiously. She shrugged. "Your cousin confirmed that I'm in a good place, something like Fort Knox."

He nodded. "Yeah, that would be her standard comment." Jasper added, with a smile, "She calls it that all the time."

"I won't argue the point, and obviously, if it's secure, then I'm happy to be here."

"It's secure," he declared, with a vehement nod.

"And then," she murmured, "what are the chances that it's fireproof?"

"It's built out of concrete," he shared, with a note of amusement. "So, it's got clay floor tiles, and the walls are concrete, as are the subfloors."

"Seriously?" she asked, staring at him in astonishment.

He nodded. "Seriously."

"Okay then, so I'm here for a day or two." And then she winced. "I can't stay much longer than that. I'll have to find another place to live."

"We'll worry about that later," he suggested. "In the meantime, you need to heal first."

"First?" she muttered, with a headshake. "I hear you, but it won't stop my mind from spinning around, wondering what I'm supposed to do from here on out."

"Of course not," he noted, "and we both want answers."

"Obviously. Who wouldn't? I just keep thinking about what I've been through." She turned to look at him. "Now, I know a lot is going on with Mason's case and all, but is somebody at least analyzing my video of the two men in the hospital?"

"I handed it off to the investigators, but I also gave it to

Tesla just now."

"Tesla? She shouldn't be doing any investigative work right now," Amber noted.

"It's what she does. She's a programmer, one of the best in the world. Plus it takes her mind off Mason for a bit," Jasper added, "so you best let her worry about that."

"Maybe she should be living here in your Fort Knox," she suggested, staring at him, "because she's the one who's a sitting duck."

"Don't you worry. She and Mason are under guard at all times," he shared. "I won't let anything happen to my cousin. She and her father and her son, Sebastian, are the last blood relatives I've got," he noted, with a smile. "And she's pretty special."

Amber didn't know the woman but from what Amber had seen at the hospital and what she had read from her computer search on the couple. She would certainly not argue with Jasper's assessment. And, if Jasper was half as loving and caring toward Tesla as he has been to Amber, then Tesla had a nice deal going, as far as her family went. Hell, Amber wanted some of that for herself.

Almost as if he had read her mind, he asked her, "Do you have any family?"

"None that I'm close to. I've got aunts and uncles, but I haven't seen them since I was young," she replied. "Like you, I don't have much for close family anymore."

"I'm sorry. That's not easy."

"No, it's not, but, after a certain amount of time, it becomes normal for you. You learn to do everything by yourself. When you don't have family, you don't miss what you don't have," she explained. "Maybe if I needed help, I could reach out and get it from my aunts and uncles, or maybe not. They are growing older, and I've never tested it," she admitted. "I've always been independent, and I prefer to keep it that way."

He smiled, then nodded. "Yeah, I hear you. I've got the same hang-ups. Once you're independent, you want to stay independent. You don't want to end up asking for help if you don't need to. However, sometimes I think that may be more of a negative than a positive."

"Maybe," she acknowledged, with a shrug. "It's not exactly something I can do anything about right now. I'm not about to reach out and ask for help in this situation. I'm sure I can find a place to live. The determining factor will be its availability. Otherwise, it's not that involved. I don't have any furniture to move now anyway," she muttered, frowning.

"Do you carry renter's insurance?"

Her eyebrows popped up, as she nodded. "I do, so that is a good thing."

"It is," he agreed, "so we can deal with that in a couple days too. "You'll need to start the process for a claim, but, other than that, you should be good to go."

She looked around the sunroom carefully, then her face relaxed into a smile, and he knew that she would let the thought go for now. "Any chance of food?"

He hopped up. "Absolutely."

"I can cook if you want," she offered, shifting to stand up. He turned and glared at her. She raised both hands and said, "Hey, I don't want to be useless."

"Not useless," he corrected. "You're hurt and healing. Temporarily you need a hand, so accept the help and don't be stubborn. Just sit here and enjoy the sun for a bit." And, with that, he turned away and entered the kitchen, heading to the stove and the fridge. Stunned, she watched, as he very efficiently prepared eggs, toast, and even bacon for an extra treat.

When he sat down again with her, bringing their breakfast into the sunroom to eat, she smiled and asked, "Are you always this perfect? A man who can look after a woman, cook, and be protective?" she pointed out, as she rolled her eyes. "Sounds like the perfect recipe for a romance novel hero."

He burst out with that now-familiar booming laugh. "If that were the case," he replied, giving her a smirk, "I would have found somebody who would take me on a long time ago."

"I've been meaning to ask what's wrong with you that you haven't got a partner."

"I'll turn that question around and ask you the same thing."

She nodded. "Touché. I work too much."

"So do I," he stated, with a laugh. "So, it sounds to me that we have a lot more in common than you thought. We both work a lot."

She smiled. "Tesla told me something about how you tend to go after what you want and rarely take no for an answer."

He shrugged. "Only if what I want also wants me back," he clarified. "If I have to pressure or force someone to want me, the allure would be gone. I would never do that."

"I know you wouldn't. I didn't mean it like that." Smiling, she added, "If this is Fort Knox, does that mean you can leave me alone here?"

He nodded. "I have to admit that was part of my thinking, yes," he confirmed, with a smile. "Not that I get out of keeping an eye on you myself and only depending on the security system," he pointed out, with a big grin, "but—"

"No, no buts," she interrupted. "It's important that you solve this. Maybe other people will be a help, but I hesitate to trust anyone else or to depend on them too much. They are just these nameless faces, and I have no way to know who can be trusted. At least I feel like I know you, so please do what you need to do. If you feel I'm safe here, go off and do whatever you can to solve this."

"I will. As soon as we're done with breakfast, I'll take off for a bit, and I'll make sure you have phone numbers in case you need anything," he added, with a quick glance at her. "I can also phone in to the system here and talk to you through that."

"Without a phone here?" she asked in fascination.

He grinned. "Exactly, without a phone."

CHAPTER 10

J ASPER LEFT SOON afterward, first making certain that Amber understood how the security system worked and that she wouldn't go outside because he had the house locked down. If she wanted to go out, he would take her as soon as he got back. In the meantime, she should do as much resting and healing as she could. He understood that could be hard work, given the fact that she was wide awake and not wanting to sleep anymore. However, she had the TV and her laptop, and she could phone various friends, although nobody could come over without Jasper disarming the alarm system, and she had agreed that was probably best not to do that for the moment.

As he went to his vehicle, he contacted Tesla and let her know what he was doing. "Are you sure you should?" she asked nervously. "That poor woman needs to be with someone."

"She's fine, and she's safe in the house, as you well know. Not to mention that it's hard for anybody to get in or out."

"I know," Tesla conceded, "but still, she must be nervous."

"She seems to be handling this pretty decently, so I'm

not sure," he stated calmly. "I won't be gone all day, but I do need to check in with the other investigators on the team. They've been awfully slow on the email responses and whatnot."

"They don't want you involved," she declared in a dry tone, "much less in a leadership role."

"Exactly, so they need to know that I'm still here, that I'm still in their face, and that I won't be stepping back just because they're willing me away," he declared, with a fury in his tone. "Now I'll go pick up lunch for the two of us before I go back home. Do you want anything special?"

"That sounds like a lovely idea," Tesla replied. "As much as I appreciate all the care and attention I'm getting here—"

"The hospital food sucks. … I know."

She burst out laughing. "Oh, it is good to laugh," she admitted, when her chuckle wound down. "You don't realize how much of a stress all this is."

"Still no change in Mason's condition?"

"No, though I keep thinking there is. … I keep thinking he's responding, and then the doctors tell me that he's in too deep."

"Don't you listen to them," Jasper stated. "He hears you. He is reaching out to you. Absolutely no way he isn't listening to you, so you talk to him all you want. You tell him exactly what he's supposed to do, which is to get his ass back beside you."

She chuckled again. "I haven't been listening to them," she confirmed, with a force in her tone that he was used to hearing. "I've felt fairly strongly about keeping a hand on him, talking to him, and I haven't had a chance to do much other than that. However, at the stage we are at, he needs to hear me, even if he's still comatose." She took a deep breath.

"I want to check out more of that video," she murmured. "Something in it caught my eye."

"Good. Take another look, and maybe you'll have information for me when I pop in with the food," he suggested, and he quickly rang off.

Twenty minutes later Jasper walked into the investigative offices. Almost immediately the noise died down around him, and everyone stopped what they were doing. He looked at them and nodded. "You all seem surprised to see me."

They shrugged. "Not sure why that would be, but we haven't seen you in a little bit."

"That's because the nurse who took the video at the hospital was injured in a hit-and-run." When they sat back in shock, he nodded. "I moved her to my place because somebody was sitting outside her place, watching her. Then they followed us, when I did get her out of there."

"You let them?" Sam asked in a mocking tone.

Jasper completely ignored him, turning to look at Morgan and said, "So, obviously something more is here with her that we need to connect with."

"I did go through the video," he admitted, "but not a whole lot there."

"Yet something is somewhere, as her place was torched after we left."

Shocked silence filled the room.

"I haven't had a chance to see it on my computer, just on my phone," Jasper shared. "So I'll pop over and take a good look at the crime scene right now."

"I'll come with you," Morgan said, and the temperature around the room dropped a few more degrees, as people exchanged glances.

Sam called out, "Yeah, the rest of us will just keep working on the Mason case then."

At the doorway, Jasper turned, standing firm and square. "I'm not sure what your problem is," he replied, with a hardness that surprised even himself, "but you can lose that attitude anytime." And with that, he stepped out and walked away.

Morgan raced to catch up. "Hey, take it easy on him. He's just not impressed that you joined the investigation as it is. We're all on the same team here."

Jasper shrugged. "I have somebody else joining this investigation too."

"What's wrong with us?" Morgan asked, a thread of defensiveness and anger winding through his tone.

"In an investigation like this, where we don't have the time and we don't have the manpower, the sooner we get this solved, the better for all of us. Don't you agree?"

"Sure, but so far all our cameras haven't captured very much."

"That's another concern. Did you track the vehicle at the sniper site?"

"We tracked six vehicles, and every one of them ended up in warehouses unloading, and we lost sight of the drivers inside, so it's as if they knew."

"Because they did," Jasper snapped, glaring at Morgan. "Either the sniper is somebody on base or somebody who has been stationed here before."

"We've searched far and wide," Morgan stated. "We're going through active personnel right now, for anybody who was in that area during those hours. Plus, we're double-checking references and alibis."

"That's great." Jasper nodded in agreement. "That's a start, but how many hours and days have gone by since

Mason was shot, and we haven't made any progress?"

"That's one of the reasons why Sam is upset," Morgan explained in frustration. "We got reamed out this morning, pretty good."

At that Jasper stopped and nodded. "I guess that's to be expected, isn't it?"

"Maybe, but we don't like it, and it's not what we want."

"Of course not," Jasper declared, with an eye roll. "None of us want to get told that we can't do our job and that we need to do it faster." Jasper understood the frustration and the lack of progress in this case were bound to tighten the already stretched nerves of these investigators, "but that is a fact of life right now. … As it is, everybody is looking at us for answers, and we haven't got any. Instead we've got more shit happening."

"What's Mason's condition?" Morgan asked.

"He's still in a coma, and won't be out of it for awhile."

"Yeah, that's done on purpose to help him to heal," he muttered.

"Send me any of the statements you have and alibis that have been double-checked," Jasper ordered. "I'll take a look for any loopholes."

"I can't do that," Morgan argued.

"I think you can, and you will," Jasper declared.

Morgan hesitated, then added, "We're also going through the backgrounds of anybody who may have had a problem with Mason."

"And given his long history on base and considering all the missions and takedowns his teams have been involved in, that could be fairly substantial."

"Absolutely, and it is," Morgan stated. "We're already into several thousand pages' worth. Everybody says he is a great guy, but he's got a lot of enemies."

"He's a great guy if you're the honest person who likes to work and if you show up to do the job," Jasper clarified, "and if you do your job well. However, if you're a shyster, a thief, or somebody who can't be trusted, then Mason is your worst enemy." Jasper sent a sharp look over at Morgan. "Keep that in mind when you look at the list of people who have anything against Mason."

"I did notice that," he conceded, with a nod. "Out of the many people he's had issues with, some of them have been kicked out, and some of them have even done time. Mason has got quite a list of people who don't like him, but they all seem to be people he either didn't get along with or were passed over for promotions."

"That always pisses people off, but you've got to be severely pissed off to kill somebody over something like a promotion or a bad review."

"In some cases, maybe they are pissed off enough. I don't know. All I can tell you is that, right now, we're still going through everybody's statements."

"That's why I asked you to send me what you've got, so I can read through it as well."

"Will do, and, for now, … just ignore Sam."

"I won't ignore Sam," Jasper argued, raising a hand in protest, "because his attitude sucks. So, he can stop that attitude, or I'll do my best to get his ass kicked off this team."

"Don't do that, please. He brings skill to the table, and he's been here a very long time, so he knows people. His nose is just out of joint."

"Then talk to him," Jasper declared. "Straighten him out and tell him to pull it back. Otherwise I will." He stated it simply and with a smile, but the threat was obvious in his tone. "You guys are down a boss man right now, aren't you?"

"Yeah, we are," Morgan replied warily.

Jasper asked him, "Will you be it?"

"I've been in it in an 'acting' capacity. I haven't decided whether I want to pursue it or not."

"I'm bringing Masters on to this investigation. Do you know him?"

"No, I don't know him at all." Morgan stared. "Is that his first name or his last name?"

"Masters is his first name. *Masters Woodrow*. He's not a guy to mess with."

"Yeah, I would be the same if my name was *Masters Woodrow* too," he replied, with a laugh. "You're bringing him on?"

"We need to get some movement here, so you can bet I'll be bringing on everybody we need," Jasper stated. "Plus, I've got this other case with the nurse, which must be connected, but I haven't found the link yet. So it's also a pain in the ass."

"So you're working the nurse case just because?"

"I'm doing that because, one, she's somebody in trouble. Two, she's been helping Tesla, and three, she's the one who took the video of the two suspicious men in the ER waiting room for me, and we saw how well that's gone for her."

"No, it's not gone well at all," Morgan agreed. "So it's guilt that has you working her case."

"No, concern," he countered, with a headshake. "I think the two guys she videoed are connected to our sniper and ran her down and then set fire to her apartment. I just need to find the link. So, she's going nowhere, until I can get a handle on this."

"But if somebody burned down her apartment intentionally ..."

"Yeah, it's more than personal for the guys who went this far. I've got a call out for any street cameras for the bulk of last night, for both her apartment and for us heading to my house. We had some asshole sitting outside her place, and then, when we left in the dark, we were followed. I lost the tail, but ..."

"There's always a *but* in there somewhere, isn't there?"

"Unfortunately that's true. I saw the one man on stakeout, and I lost the tail, but I don't know whether it was the same man or not. I also don't know whether somebody just replaced him or they got pissed off and just took down her apartment as a warning or were hoping that maybe she'd been left behind."

"That will be a very sloppy scene then," Morgan noted. "I don't understand that."

"Yep, me neither, unless the guy just has a short fuse. However, I won't assume anything at this point. If you can get the rest of the cameras from her street and all the others at the hospital, where she was run down, we just may get a hit."

"All of them?" Morgan asked.

"Yeah, I'm looking for a specific vehicle sitting outside her house. A small two-door Honda, red."

"Red is a hard color to hide, so I would be surprised if that's what they were doing," Morgan replied cautiously.

"You and me both, but maybe that's why he did it. All I can tell you is that's the vehicle that sat outside, and then ... this one tailed me." He pulled up his phone and showed him the picture. "A silver Camry. Amber said the car that ran her down was a gray vehicle."

"Crap," Morgan muttered, "you had a busy night."

"I had a very busy night, and I'm pretty pissed off, so I'm not looking for too much more sass from anybody," Jasper declared, with a look back at the room behind them.

"I'll talk to Sam," Morgan stated.

"You do that." Jasper headed for the exit.

Morgan stopped Jasper, offering, "I'll be your legs and go check out the fire scene, take photos, share them with you. One less thing you need to do."

Jasper studied Morgan, then nodded. "I'll hit the street cams."

And, with that, Jasper headed back into the department, toward the room he was using as an office, and closed the door, finally giving himself some peace and quiet to sit down and to get some work done. He ordered the relevant cams to be sent to him. Next he would check out that video Amber had made on the department's big-screen TV. It would give him a clearer and crisper image than anything on his phone, his tablet or his laptop. Something had to be on there. Something they were all missing to date. He would compare notes with Tesla later, after he studied it further himself.

He pulled it up on the monitor and then, using the technology available, put it up on the big screen in front of him. He got up, walked over and slowly, frame by frame, went over it. Tesla had mentioned how she'd seen something, so what did she see?

He wished she'd given him a hint, so he had something to go on as a starting place, and then it hit him. He leaned forward, and it wasn't so much about the two guys in the foreground of the video that Amber had been specifically recording, but the lone guy standing in the background. His cap was pulled down low, his hands in his pockets, and he was leaning up against the wall, but his gaze shifted as he watched. His gaze went everywhere and then finally landed on her. He had immediately stiffened—aware she was videotaping him—and changed his position so his face was more concealed.

Jasper went to his laptop, cut that frame out, and contacted Tesla. "The guy in the background in the waiting room."

"Yeah, that's the one I was thinking of," she confirmed.

"We need his face. What about the hospital cameras? We might get a full-on view of his face."

"Maybe," she muttered. "Have you got permission?"

"The team should have. However, I want to see the security footage myself," he stated bluntly.

"Good, then you run through it, see if you can get me a cleaner picture," Tesla said, "and I'll run that through the database."

"Do you recognize anything about him?" he asked.

"No, and Mason isn't awake to ask."

"He will be," Jasper declared. "You just keep focused and don't let this sideline you."

"Ha, that won't happen," she stated, with a chuckle, "but you get me a photo I can use because this one just won't be clear enough to match."

"I'm on it. Don't you worry. I'm on it." He disconnected, then looked up the hospital board members and made a quick phone call, asking for permission for the security cameras. This time he used his title and his investigative status. When he got the permission almost immediately, he smiled.

An awful lot to be said for having clearance. He logged in, headed back to the expected date and time, and, sure enough, saw the same scene unfolding that Amber had recorded but from a slightly different angle. For several different angles, he brought up multiple cameras. He split the screen and put them up on the big monitor in front of him.

Morgan walked in later and went rigid as he saw the screens. "Wow, which one are you interested in here?"

"This one." Jasper tapped the face. "When Amber was taking the video, she was initially focused in on these two guys in the foreground, who appeared to be having an intense conversation. However, I don't think they had anything to do with Mason's case. Yet our initial focus led us to this guy in the background." He pointed out the guy in the back and added, "Watch." He hit Play and then slowly moved it forward frame by frame.

Morgan whistled. "I think you're right. He's hiding from the cams."

"When I go back earlier on the security cams from the hospital, he arrived just before the ambulance with Mason, and only one way for him to have known the ambulance was on the way."

Morgan grimaced. "Right, if he knew Mason was coming in."

"The only way to have known that was if he had something to do with the sniper shots at Mason."

TESLA RESPONDED TO the phone message and the snippets of videos that kept coming in from Jasper. She studied them intently, looking to see where and what. It didn't take long for her to patch from internal hospital videos to external cams focused on the parking area and catch sight of the vehicle the guy arrived in.

She quickly phoned Jasper. "I caught the vehicle outside that he came in," she said, by way of a greeting. "I just barely got the license plate." She quickly rattled it off.

"I'm on it. Was it a silver Camry by any chance?"

"Yes." She froze. "How did you know?"

"That vehicle tailed us last night."

"Damn," she whispered, "so you think he's the one who torched Amber's apartment?"

"I don't know. He might have come back and done it just out of temper."

"Asshole," she muttered.

He chuckled. "And Mason?"

"Mason is just the same," she muttered, glancing at the bed where her husband slept.

"So, the docs aren't saying anything?"

"No, other than he needs more time to heal, thus the medically induced coma," she repeated, with a biting tone, "and I'm trying not to let it get to me."

"Good," Jasper replied, understanding, not minding her mood swings at all. "Sometimes the doctors get it wrong. And yet they could be right to give him more time. Better more time than not enough. Let's not worry about it right now."

"No, … I'm not planning on it. I trust that Mason is coming back to me," she stated, tears coming to her eyes, and now sniffling. "That's all I can do."

"You don't have to trust anything. You already know inside that he would do whatever it takes to be there for you. So give it a little bit of time, and you'll be just fine."

Only after she hung up did she relax and whisper,

"Come on, Mason. Pull through this, please."

Almost as if by magic, she swore she saw him shift just the slightest. She raced to his bedside, then kissed him. "Hey, anytime you want to wake up, I'll be happy to see you."

She waited, cuddled him a little bit longer, still seeing no change. Then she gave a hard sigh and sat back down again.

One of the nurses walked in just then. She immediately noted Tesla's downcast expression. "Don't be depressed. We've seen a lot of patients come through this."

Tesla looked up at her and smiled. "I don't know if that's such a good thing to say," she murmured, "because I would like to think that this doesn't happen all that much."

"Unfortunately it does, but this is a healing coma, as far as we can see. We don't have any reason to worry that he's been in any way hurting or that he is having an abnormal reaction."

Tesla nodded and watched as the nurse went through the regular routine of checking him over. Tesla had met with Sasha, and the operating room doctor, on the second day that Mason was down. Tesla needed to get a feel for exactly what the nurses should be doing versus not doing with her husband. Sasha had been so thorough about setting forth the proper routine that Tesla should look for with each nurse. So far, absolutely nothing had set off Tesla's warning bells, but she couldn't take the chance that something might happen as soon as she let her guard down.

So Tesla at least did her best to always be awake or to alert one of the two guards outside Mason's room. She couldn't guarantee that she always knew whether or not somebody came in. Hopefully the guards took note if Tesla had nodded off and stepped in with each nurse, just to be sure. Tesla was determined to keep watch, no matter the hardship on her, just as long as Mason was left alone to heal and to come back to her.

She wiped away the sleep from her eyes. She couldn't sleep here in the same way. She was tired. She was worn out, and it just never seemed to change. She loved this man to the end of the earth. Mason was her everything, and seeing him like this was breaking her up. She shifted position and relaxed, grateful that Jasper was on the investigation. Sad that it took something like this to get him to jump back into the field where he excelled, but she understood his hesitancy after such a personal betrayal. Tesla was glad that something good came out of his pain.

After once bitten by a betrayal, such as Jasper had experienced, it was no wonder he had hesitated to dive back into his investigative work. Tesla imagined how Jasper must have created a certain amount of distance from that betrayal, while on leave. Surely the memories still taunted him, a remnant of everything that had gone wrong before. He must be forever looking to keep a delicate balance between not judging something in a way that wasn't fair, maintaining his healthy skepticism, and yet rebuilding the ability to trust, even in his own abilities and instincts.

Tesla knew that was partly why Jasper had held off jumping back into work. He'd had weeks if not months off, certainly more than he needed to recover physically. She'd lost track of time, she had to admit, but he was such a damn good person and so good at his job that she wanted him here, wanted him helping. Still, it frustrated her that absolutely nobody could find anything on the sniper yet.

She knew certain areas of the base had been searched and security footage reviewed. She heard that they had tracked several vehicles to warehouses, then followed up on each.

One vehicle escaping the sniper scene area had been found empty and abandoned on a road somewhere. Of course the car had been stolen anyway, so that was a complete dead end. She didn't know about this Camry that kept coming up and trusted that somebody would get back to her with the information on its owner and the possible current GPS position on the car. But the waiting? … Damn it to hell, waiting was hard.

MASON SHIFTED ONCE again in the bed.

All he could do was run. It seemed like he'd been running for weeks. He was getting away from some asshole, and somehow it kept leading him back to Tesla. He would do anything to save Tesla, so no way he would let this asshole get close to her. She was everything good in this world, even if Mason didn't deserve her. No way he would let somebody like *him* come after her. The fact that anybody was even after her scared the crap out of Mason because he didn't understand why.

Why would someone be after Tesla?

Something was wrong with this whole picture. He moaned, wishing for something to ease the pain, but he didn't even know where the pain was coming from. It kept breaking into his world and shifting him from his focus, and that just pissed him off too. So rare for him to have pain to the point that he couldn't control his reaction to it. Therefore, he didn't know what the hell was wrong this time.

But every time he tried to blank it out or to move past it, something dragged him back under again. Frustrating, infuriating, and so not like him.

He stopped and turned to look around once more, wondering if he was still being followed. *There.* Sure enough, just as he turned, he saw the stranger duck behind the corner too. Swearing, Mason turned, and, instead of going home, he detoured once again into the shadows, always leading the pursuer away from Tesla and his three-year-old son. No way in hell he was bringing danger home to them.

CHAPTER 11

AMBER FELL ASLEEP, surfaced, and realized where she was. The thought of Fort Knox had her feeling safe again for the first time in days. She rolled over and went back to sleep again. She woke the next time to a weird *ping* on her phone. She must have an email or a text. Picking up her phone, she checked the new email message, frowning at it. *You wanted him. You got him.* She didn't know what the hell that meant, and she sat up, noting an attachment to the email.

It couldn't load on her phone, and that frustrated her. She snagged her laptop, wondering if she should even be opening any attachment from this unknown sender. With so many viruses out there, that was definitely a concern, yet she brought up the email. As the image revealed itself, she stared at it in horror. She quickly reached for her phone again and called Jasper.

He seemed distracted when he answered.

"It's me," she said urgently. "I just forwarded you an email. Please tell me it's not what I think it is."

"Hold on. Hold on," he replied, taking full note of her panic. "Let me bring it up. When did you get it?"

"Like two minutes ago. It woke me up from a nap."

"That was crappy timing," he noted in a conversational tone. "Here it is. The picture is not quite … holy shit."

Her heart sank, and she pinched the bridge of her nose. "Please tell me it's not what I think it is."

"I'm not sure what you think it is, but it seems to be our mystery man, the one who you saw in the hospital, right?"

"Yes, and you and I both know what that photo means."

"Unfortunately I do," he agreed, with a sigh. "Even more unfortunate is that I'm pretty sure that's the alley behind my house. Stay where you are. Do not go to the door. Do not answer your phone." When she didn't answer him right away, he snapped, "Do you hear me?"

"I hear you. I'm not doing anything. I'm just sitting here, waiting."

"You won't have to wait very long. I'll be there as fast as I can."

She heard him call out to somebody in the distance with a quick explanation, but he was still on the phone with her. "Good. I'll wait. You can disconnect now."

"For my sake, I want you to stay on the line, and I'll keep up a conversation with you the whole way home. That okay with you?"

Her stomach knotted. "Do you think I'm in danger?"

"No, I don't, but it will make me feel better." She snorted at that. "What? You don't think I'm worried about you? You would be wrong. I'm very worried, and right now this is not what I want to see."

"I don't think it's what anybody wants to see, and I highly doubt the dead guy on the ground in this photo wanted this to happen either."

"No, and I get that," he muttered. "So, we've got quite a situation on the go, and I have a team coming with me right now.”

“Should I put on coffee?”

“No. I don’t trust a couple investigators here, and I haven’t had a chance to fully clear them yet.”

“But they’re part of the team?” she cried out.

“Yes, part of the existing team. However, I’m putting together my own team. The only person I’m bringing on board myself to date is Masters, and he’s doing a bunch of running around for me as it is. If I can get him on the investigative part of the team, it will make me happier.”

“Crap,” she muttered. “Don’t you trust anybody?”

“Right now, I don’t trust anybody, and neither should you.”

“What about trusting you?” she asked, half joking.

“If I was anybody but me, … I would say don’t trust me either. However, right now you must trust somebody, so it better be me.”

“Good God,” she muttered, as she sagged back onto the couch.

“Are you downstairs?”

“Yes,” she replied, yet still distracted by his previous comment. “Are you saying I can’t trust you?”

“No, of course I’m not saying that. It should be obvious by now that you can trust me.”

“Yeah, right up until you say shit like that.”

“I’m on my way and in the vehicle, so hold tight.”

“And are you still keeping the phone open?”

“Yes, I’m keeping the line open.”

“See? That just scares me even more,” she muttered, “because, if you weren’t panicked, you wouldn’t be keeping the phone open.”

“It’s just a precaution. I want to ensure that nobody is

coming after you."

"How could they? You told me that this place is Fort Knox."

"And it is," he confirmed, "but you never know what assholes are out there right now. I never saw this coming. Did you?"

"No, of course I didn't," she cried out.

"You do recognize him, I presume?"

"I recognize him from the hospital, yes," she said, "but I don't recognize him in terms of this being somebody I'm supposed to know. I don't know who he is or anything about him."

"Good. By the way, I'm coming in with a guy named Morgan. He's part of the existing team."

"Yeah, the good part or the bad part?"

He chuckled, and she heard another man on the other end.

"The good part, definitely the good part," Morgan stated in frustration. "Why in the hell would you even say that to her?"

"Because I haven't had a chance to clear you guys yet," Jasper shared, with a chuckle.

"I told you that I had an alibi."

"You did, but again I haven't had a chance to clear it."

"Crap, no wonder the other guys get pissed at you."

"They can get pissed off all they want," Jasper declared, his tone hardening very rapidly. "It doesn't make a damn bit of difference to me because I only work with those who are telling the truth. So let's hope that nobody slipped out for coffee and did anything that impacts this investigation in any way."

"You know we aren't working for you, right?"

"Yeah, I understand how you all think that," he replied, with a knowing smile in his tone.

She listened to the conversation, wondering at the undertones and whether this Morgan guy understood that Jasper had already decided that Morgan and his team had no say in the matter. She wasn't even sure how that worked. In her department, changes like that were often made in the ER without anybody being aware, and it caused confusion and disgruntled conflicts all the time. Maybe that was happening here with Morgan, she didn't know.

When Jasper spoke again, he told her, "We're just pulling up into the yard. I'm going around to the back."

"Fine, you go there first. Maybe we've just been deceived by a costume party back there."

"Not likely," Jasper argued. "I'll end the call now. If you hear people out in the backyard, it's me." Then he disconnected. She sat here and waited and waited, wondering just what the hell she was supposed to do now.

When her phone rang again, Jasper said, "Hang tight. I'm coming inside through the back door." Just then she heard the alarm speak, saying the system was being disarmed.

"Please tell me that's you."

"It's me," he confirmed, "and I have Morgan with me."

"If you say so," she muttered, and suddenly he was there in front of her. She bolted off the couch, almost falling with the pain of it, when he caught her.

"Whoa, you shouldn't move so fast just yet," he muttered, then gave her a big kiss that caught her completely by surprise. When she turned around, he was grinning at the stranger in the room. "This," he began, rounding her to face the other guy, "is Amber. Amber, this is Morgan."

"Hi, Morgan," she said, as Jasper led her back to the

couch. She looked up at him, willing to forget about the kiss for the moment, as she wanted to know what he'd found. "Please tell me that was a ghastly joke."

He grimaced and shook his head. "No joke," he replied softly.

Tears came to her eyes, and she shook her head. "Dear God," she whispered. "Why?"

"Probably because he got caught," Morgan suggested. "So, somebody is cleaning up potential loose ends, and he seemed to have drawn the short straw."

She gasped in horror. "So, you're saying that I'm responsible for this man's death?"

"No, you're not responsible at all," Jasper corrected, taking her hand and giving it a squeeze. "You don't need to take on that guilt. It's not your fault at all. The dead man made choices that he probably wouldn't make again, if he knew what the outcome would be, but that is not your fault."

She swallowed hard and nodded. On some level, she understood what he was saying, but the fact of the matter was, if she hadn't called attention to him, he would probably still be alive today. She wrapped her arms around her chest and looked back and forth between them. "Now what?"

"Forensics is on their way, and we have a team working the scene right now."

"Are they in the yard?" she asked.

"No, they are in the surrounding area. I own that property too," he noted, with a shrug. "So they're searching that section. We're still on the inside of the gate." She just nodded. Jasper turned to address Morgan. "We'll need to interview the neighbors."

"I'm on it," he replied, starting for the door. He smiled, as he looked back at her. "Nice to meet you." Then he quickly left.

She looked over at Jasper. "Was that kiss a proprietary thing?"

"No, an attempt to let him know that you were okay, that you can be trusted."

"Ha, he won't necessarily believe that."

"Maybe not," Jasper admitted, with a grin, "but anything that eases the pressure right now is a help."

"If you say so," she muttered. "Right now it just feels as if everything is so damn wrong. Why would they have killed him?"

"Because he was seen," he repeated simply. "I told you that."

"People don't kill for that."

"These guys do. Obviously if the stakes are high enough, they can't take a chance that we can link the dead man back to the other bad guys involved here."

She swallowed, then nodded. "That picture will haunt me forever."

"I understand where you're coming from, but the guilt is not yours here," he said carefully. "Think of your ER work. Does every dead patient make you feel guilty?"

She wrinkled up her face and grimaced.

"Maybe that guilt must be part of your genetic makeup that led you to be a nurse, to be a healer. Probably nothing I can do about that because you won't believe it when we say it's not your fault, but it isn't. If he wasn't involved, then he wouldn't have ended up like this."

"How was he killed?"

"Single bullet to the back of the head."

She winced. "So, like an execution."

He nodded with interest. "I suppose you pick up that

stuff in your work, don't you?"

"Yeah, whether I like it or not, it's just become a part of the business. We also talk to the cops a fair bit, so I guess the terminology comes across."

"Of course," he murmured. "It's probably just as well you're not going back to work right away, even after your days off."

"And is that your call or mine?" she asked coolly.

"Neither. More of a medical nature, for you individually and for those around you. One, you're still sidelined with a bum leg, and two, it's obvious that you still present a problem for somebody. And three, because this guy's been killed, I'm a little concerned about you taking that danger to the hospital."

She grimaced at that. "That's an argument killer right there," she conceded, as she stared at him in sorrow. "That's the last thing I would want."

"I know that. So, for the moment, just follow my lead, okay?"

"Yeah, sure," she muttered, with an eye roll, "and I suppose it comes with a whole pile of kisses."

"Why? Was the kiss a bad deal?" he asked, but his lips were twitching.

She glared at him. "That's not funny."

"Sorry, I figure any humor right now can only help ease a difficult time. So, I am sorry if that's not working for you, but it's one of the methods I've often used to get through these situations."

With that, she realized just how much he had probably seen in his life. "I see the other side of it," she shared, "but you're right. Humor is often a way for us to get through it, and I'm sorry too. … I promise that I'm not trying to be difficult.”

He shook his head. “Point taken, and, fair enough, we’re both upset over this.”

“At least now you’ll find out who he is.”

“I will, and we also know that he arrived at the hospital just ahead of Mason’s ambulance.”

Her jaw dropped. “Oh my God, the hospital cameras helped you to figure that out?”

“They did,” he stated, “and I did get permission, in case you’re wondering.”

“Right, of course you did. Sorry, I don’t know what I was thinking.”

“Yet,” he added, “we still need to find out who else is associated with the dead man and the sniper and whether he has any military background because, from there, hopefully we can access a lot of other information.”

“I hope so. Is it just me or is everything taking way too long right now?”

“Oh, it’s not just you,” he agreed. “Believe me that the brass is breathing down everybody’s neck right now. Nobody wants this violence to go any further, and, more than that, they’re all aware that the events are still escalating.”

“Right, and that’s the problem for me too.”

“Exactly. The problem is escalating with you right in the middle of it. While none of us want that to happen, it is.” When she didn’t say anything, he added, “If you’re okay for now, I’ll head outside and confirm everything is moving forward.”

She nodded. “Will you lock up afterward?”

He nodded. “Yeah, I will.”

And, with that, he was gone.

JASPER STEPPED OUTSIDE, on the doorstep, watching as the forensics people scurried around, while vehicles came and went. He looked over to see her standing a little bit behind him. "Are you sure you should be up?"

"You didn't put on the security system," she explained, "so I wasn't sure what the problem was."

"The problem is, chaos is out there, and I was keeping out of the way."

"Okay. I don't know whether you need coffee or something, but …"

"I would love a cup of coffee," he admitted, nodding solemnly, "if you are up to putting it on."

She nodded, then moved slowly into the kitchen. He turned back to the chaos on the other side of the fence. When his phone rang, he noted Morgan was calling. "Hey," he replied in a rush. "What's the report?"

"So, a single shot, just the one bullet in the body, and no casing, at least none that we can find so far. Everybody else will stay and finish the forensics. Where do you want me to go?"

"Head back to the office," Jasper replied, without even second-guessing his instructions. "Get all the interviews into the system, so we can sort those out. We also need to track whatever vehicle dropped off the dead body."

"You probably have better security and equipment for that part than we do."

Jasper almost swore at that reminder. "I'll take a look and see if they figured out what I've got—or not—for home security. I should have that information in a few minutes."

"What about Amber? Is she okay? She didn't seem that

steady on her feet."

"She's okay. Getting hit by that car was no joke. She took quite a bump, and then her apartment got torched. Now she's just shocked with the dead body brought here. That violence is upsetting, especially when she feels responsible."

"And yet it's not her fault."

"No, it isn't, but she'll take on that guilt anyway. She's an ER nurse, and killing isn't part of her contribution to the world, but saving people is."

"Yeah, and her whole world has gone ass over teakettle in a big way," he muttered. "I see why you feel the need to keep her safe."

And, with that, Morgan rang off.

CHAPTER 12

AMBER MADE COFFEE and sat at the kitchen table, while Jasper worked on the laptop in front of her. She didn't disturb him, but she was dying to know if he had found anything.

Finally he whispered, "Gotcha," and gave her a feral grin.

"Got what?" she asked, staring at him intently. "Did you find him? What could you possibly find since he was right in the backyard?"

"Exactly," he said, a knowing smile on his face, "and he was dumped there on purpose, not killed onsite. And … I found the vehicle that dumped him."

She got up and came around to his side of the table. She was surprised at how quickly she was able to move and realized, when she wasn't focused on it, the unhindered movement came naturally. As soon as she got around, she took a look at the vehicle and nodded. "Now, that's interesting."

"What's interesting?"

"I almost feel like …"

"What?" he asked.

"I'm thinking that might be the same vehicle that ran

me down."

He nodded. "They do look similar, don't they?"

"They do," she agreed, with a confused expression, "but I didn't see the license plate."

He pulled out his notepad and stated, "It is a similar-looking car but a different license plate." He did a quick search and then gave out a *whoop*. "The license plate is for an SUV, not a small car."

"They have different plates?"

"Yes, every vehicle type has a different plate sequence," he explained, "so this could definitely be the one that ran you down."

"I was thinking they weren't trying to kill me back then. If the hit was intentional, maybe they just wanted to intimidate me."

"Agreed, but, with the subsequent apartment fire, they might have changed their minds by now," he murmured. "This is past warnings for them. They're tying up loose ends, more as a lesson, I think … for you."

"What? So, by doing that"—she pointed to the screen where the dead guy was still displayed—"they're telling me not to talk?" This all was too alien for her. "They ran me down with a car, burned down my apartment, and now they've killed somebody I filmed in the hospital?" she summed up. "What else do they think they can do now?"

"They can kill you," he declared, turning to look at her, "and that's what all this is leading up to. It's a direct threat against your life, but rest assured. They didn't kill their associate because of you or as a lesson to you, but because they would take him out anyway. They used it as a teaching point. These people kill everyone involved, so no one leads back to them."

She groaned. "God, these people are barbaric." She wrapped her arms around her chest, as she sat once more, now huddled on the opposite side of the kitchen table. She stared at him. "Might be a good time for me to take a long holiday."

"It would be," he agreed, yet giving her a headshake, "but I have no doubt that they have great ways to monitor airports—as they did for the shooting of Mason. Therefore, if you decide to fly out, they could track you to wherever it is you're going."

Her heart sank. "Seriously? Why do they even care about me?"

"They probably want the video."

Her breath instantly whooshed from her chest. "So that's it? It is about the video? Crap, I wasn't even filming him, the dead guy. … I was worried about the other two guys."

"So, yeah, I would imagine that's what it's all about," he noted, looking up at her. "However, in our digital world, surely they know that copies exist. You gave it to me. I shared it with Tesla and Morgan and others."

"Right, I did immediately share it with you."

Jasper shook his head. "I keep coming back to how the video has something important on it. Something these bad guys really don't want shared. Yet you seem to be the key factor here, no matter who else has seen that video. Maybe you saw something that didn't make it on the video? Of course you won't know that it's important to Mason's case, which will make finding it that much harder."

Amber sighed. "I've reviewed the tape over and over. I just don't see anything."

"Yeah, but you're looking from the mind of a rational nurse interested in healing people, not from the mind of criminal, trying to cover up more crimes. Is it still on your phone?"

She nodded.

"Then get rid of it," he ordered, making a quick decision. "We have copies, so you don't need it on your phone."

She pulled out her phone and frowned. "I can't tell them that I deleted it, and they won't give a crap anyway, since I could have sent copies all over." Then she gasped. "They can't allow me to live. I'm another loose end to tie up. They'll take me down regardless," she shared bitterly. "You think that too, don't you?"

"I don't have a whole lot of choice but to consider that," he murmured, not liking that she had put this together so fast, "but I won't lie to you. Clearly they're not playing games now," he shared, as he looked out toward his backyard. "It's gone well past that point. That's why we've got to find them and lock them up."

"In the meantime, I'm a target. *Great*," she muttered. "So now what?"

"Now we'll dissect the dead guy's life, figure out who these other people are who are still threatening you, how they discovered you, and how they connect to Mason."

"Oh." She stopped and frowned, as he mentioned Mason's name. "It's connected to Mason?"

"It's got to be connected in some way. I just don't know to what extent. It's possible this guy they killed was a random factor, and they hired him, maybe a local, just to get the information they needed about Mason's condition."

"Good Lord, so in that case he probably died for what, one hundred bucks?"

"Unfortunately it's all too possible. And, if so, then he may have seen you enter Mason's hospital room more than the other nurses, maybe even saw you conversing with Tesla."

"Crap," she muttered, as she got up and began to pace the room. "Okay, in that case, I need food first. Then I need to do something different to distract myself, like have a hot bubble bath, where I don't have to think about how people in this world can be so shitty."

"*Food*. Damn it. I was supposed to pick up food and deliver it to you and Tesla."

"It doesn't matter," she murmured. "I can just have some toast or something."

"No, I'll go get food anyway." When she shivered—from worry, not cold—he shook his head. "You'll be fine, but, if you want, I can call Morgan back to stay with you."

"No, I would rather be alone."

"I'm sorry," he muttered. "I don't want you to be afraid of being here."

"I would prefer to stay alone. I would feel safer that way. At least then I don't have to worry about being taken out by a member of your team, one you don't even trust," she muttered.

"I won't be long." He swore under his breath. "Can't believe I forgot it."

"It's fine, and it's hardly important."

He shrugged. "I can order in."

She stared up at him. "I'm not that hungry that I can't wait."

"It doesn't matter." He shook his head. "I'll take care of it." He stepped away and quickly made a couple phone calls and smiled. "I'm sending a delivery to Tesla too."

"Do you trust the delivery people?"

Jasper snorted. "Yes. They are my own people. I still

need to step outside."

Yet he hesitated still, and she waved her hand at him. "With all that crew outside, no way anybody will try to enter the house." She sighed. "I'm fine. Just go."

He leaned over, gave her a hard kiss on the lips, and took a step back to see her face flushed. "Fine." And then he was gone.

She touched her lips, wondering why that had happened. How had they gone from a causal relationship to something that required a goodbye kiss?

And yet she welcomed it. She welcomed the emotions, the feelings, the realization that maybe something in life was worth living for after all this, because right now she was feeling put upon, and that just made her feel even worse. To think that poor man died because of her just broke her heart, and the last thing she wanted was to have that memory go away.

She needed to remember that whatever this was, she was playing for keeps, and she didn't dare make a mistake and end up being one of the casualties, just like the man in the alleyway had.

JASPER STOOD OUTSIDE, just out of Amber's sight, enough that she wouldn't know whether he was here or not. He did want to survey the activity out here on his property but didn't want her to worry. He also had no intention of leaving her alone to get food. He had called on others he trusted to do that job, and, sure enough, it wasn't but minutes later when a vehicle pulled up, and Evan stepped out, a grin on his face.

He handed him several large bags as he approached him. "All yours."

"What about Tesla?"

"That's my next stop," he replied, with a smile. "I haven't had confirmation of it, but I did hear from somebody that the doctors were cautiously optimistic about Mason. Did you hear the same thing?"

Jasper shook his head. "No, I haven't heard that at all."

Evan's face fell. "Damn, I was hoping that you would give me a high five and say he was awake and doing fine."

"Can't do that yet," Jasper noted, "but, like you, I'm hoping that's the next step."

"Yeah, damn. Okay, I'll head over and talk to Tesla now, and I know. … I'll try not to upset her."

Jasper smiled. "She's gold, that girl," Jasper murmured, "no upsetting allowed."

Evan just rolled his eyes and was gone quickly.

Jasper walked back into the house and saw no sign of Amber. He knew that she was looking at having a bath and maybe that's where she'd gone. He frowned, pulled out his phone, and called her. When she answered, she seemed dazed for a minute there. "Hey, I'm downstairs with food."

"That was fast," she replied delightedly.

"Did you get into a bath?"

"No, I was just lying down."

"Good. Stay there, and I'll come up."

"No, you don't have to," she protested. "I can come down."

"Be quiet and let me make this easier on you," he said amiably.

And, with that, he hung up, stepped into the kitchen, and grabbed plates, napkins, and forks, and headed upstairs.

When he got to her room, he knocked, then opened the door. "Don't get up. Just stay where you are and relax."

He walked over, put everything down on the floor and snagged one of the small bedside tables, clearing the items on top, and brought it over to use as a temporary table.

"We'll eat in bed?" she asked.

He looked up, flashed a wicked grin in her direction, and said, "Sounds good to me. It's not the usual dinner and a date that I begin a relationship with, but it works."

She rolled her eyes at that. "You would jump at the chance, if I took you up on it."

"What makes you think that?" he asked in astonishment.

"It must have been a long time for you."

He laughed. "Hey, no derogatory remarks, please," he teased. "That's not allowed."

"But teasing is okay," she noted, with a quirk of a smile. "I have to admit that it's been a little while since I had a long-term relationship."

"Me too," he admitted, "but that doesn't mean we have to wait and put in a certain amount of time in pain and suffering before starting a new one."

"No, of course not," she agreed.

"Good, so in that case, consider this an open invitation for us to get to know each other better."

She smiled. "You do move quickly."

"No, not quickly enough," he argued. "You slept under my roof last night, and I didn't make a move at all. You might have noticed that." When she stared at him, he laughed. "Just teasing."

"No, you're not," she muttered. She scooted over to sit before the makeshift table in front of her. "Wow, what is all this?"

"Chinese. Wasn't sure what you wanted, so I got a selection." When she stared at him, he shrugged. "It seemed like the easiest thing to do."

"Thanks, but you know it's not that necessary."

"Besides, it's fun. So let me just spoil you." He opened the bags and, sure enough, removed loads of food. He pulled out several Chinese dishes and put them on the table. "I wasn't sure what you wanted, so I ordered some vegetables, some with almonds, chicken, plus noodles and rice," he shared, putting each container on the table, one by one. "I hope you like something here."

"That makes sense if you're talking strictly Chinese," she said. "I was afraid that you'd ordered Italian, Chinese, burgers, and whatever else."

"No, not at all." He smiled at her.

"But this should give us enough leftovers that we won't have to worry about food for another day or two. Good Lord, it should be enough for half a dozen people," she noted.

He smiled broadly, when her eyes widened as she looked around at all the dishes. He handed her a pair of chopsticks. "You get to start first."

"Why?" she asked suspiciously.

"So I can finish it up," he stated, with a chuckle.

"You can't seriously eat all this. No way."

He shrugged. "Hey, I'm a big guy, and I'm hungry, so you better take the offer while you can."

He watched while she opened several of the containers and served herself a decent portion. He nodded approvingly. "I do like a woman who can eat."

She laughed. "I do like my groceries," she murmured, "but I hadn't considered that was something I should be even thinking about."

"You shouldn't," he said. "That's my job, and groceries are important, particularly right now." He kept his tone jovial and calm, hoping that she wouldn't feel the need to ask any questions about what was going on outside. He held a faint hope; she was a nurse after all. She had certainly seen more-than-enough trauma in her life to recognize that some definite issues existed outside.

After she'd eaten about half of the food on her plate, she set down her fork and sighed. "That's a good start."

He laughed. "Yeah, especially for somebody who thought I brought way-too-much food."

"You did, but I do love leftovers," she noted. "Right now, I'm wondering when you'll tell me about what's going on outside."

"You already know," he murmured.

"I know that the forensics people will be there," she added. "I can't believe that nothing is happening in terms of solving this."

He stared at her in astonishment. "Just because we don't have definitive results or a culprit in handcuffs, don't think that nothing's happening. We're all working to track down the man who dropped off our dead body, checking all the city cameras, checking all known associates, running facial recognition, everything that can be done. We're doing all that, but some of it can take quite a bit of time to assimilate." He noted her bottom lip wobbled and then suddenly firmed, and he understood. "This isn't so much about *not* getting answers. It's more about the fact that this man died and that you still feel guilty."

She sniffled and nodded. "Once a little time and distance has passed, I probably won't feel the same way, but, for the moment, it's very hard to see this as anything other than my fault."

He stared at her, wondering how to convince her otherwise.

She looked over at him. "I know we've hashed it out a couple times and that, as far as you're concerned, if anybody is at fault, it's you. However, I don't see it that way, and, until this is over, it feels so very wrong."

"It *is* very wrong," he confirmed. "It's all very wrong, and I understand that the guilt is eating away at you, particularly the way they did it."

"And that's another thing," she pointed out. "They targeted me."

He sat back and nodded. "Yes. The way they dropped off the body was also a dig, almost a message to say, *Hey, you think you're hidden, but you're not*, you know? And of course, they emailed you the photo." She sucked in a breath and stared at him, and he nodded. "Just in case you hadn't seen that aspect too."

"Honestly I hadn't," she acknowledged and then stared around the room. "Are you sure we're safe here?"

"We're safe," he confirmed. "I'm not exactly sure what their next move will be or why they felt the need to do this, but a warning for you is a warning for me. It's another reason I won't be leaving you."

Then she looked at the Chinese food and back at him, nodding. "Right. Your special delivery by your own men, whom you trust."

He nodded. "Yeah, I have plenty of people running around, helping me," he explained. "So it wasn't an issue to get somebody to pick up food for us. I had food delivered to Tesla as well." He smiled, as she relaxed. Something about getting food was okay, as long as for other people, not just for her. "You have trouble accepting help, don't you?"

She blinked at the sudden change in conversation, and then she slowly nodded. "Maybe."

He reached into a container and pulled out another egg roll and put it on her plate. "No *maybe* about it." She glared at him, and he shrugged. "Be honest. You help others, but you have trouble accepting help."

"Maybe," she repeated, and hearing the word coming out of her mouth again, she laughed.

"It does seem to be a common word for you," he murmured.

"I think it's just that, when you're put on the spot, you do anything you can to deflect interest."

"Absolutely," he agreed, a bright grin on his face, "and I'll let you continue to deflect interest, at least for a little while."

She shook her head. "Do you think all this surrounding me is personal?"

"No, I don't. I think it's definitely all connected to Mason, but we can't ignore the fact that there could be some crossover involved as well."

WELL AFTER THE Chinese food had been cleared up and Amber had had another nap, she sat in the living room with him. And then she admitted, "I didn't delete that video."

She brought it up and played it in front of him, memorizing it, and taking a last look to see if anything else was important. He looked over at her, and she felt the intensity of his gaze, as she watched the video once more. She frowned at one point, as she recognized that more people were involved. Then she backed it up slowly and watched again.

"What is it that you see?" he asked.

"At one point in time it seems our dead man is talking to Dr. Charles," she shared, taking yet another look.

Jasper got up and sat on the couch beside her, as she replayed that part.

He frowned. "All I see is part of a white coat, the back of it. How do you know which doctor this is?"

She pointed at the edge of the video. "Watch him turn his head here." After a moment or two, she said, "That mole behind his ear tells me this is Dr. Charles."

"Okay. So do you think that would be unusual for Dr. Charles to speak to someone in the ER hallway?"

She pondered that. "If somebody managed to catch him in the ER and talked to him, I could see it. Other than that, generally he's pretty unavailable. He's in the OR suite or in his office, dictating notes for the medical files."

Jasper frowned. "That doesn't mean a whole lot to me. So, what does that mean to you?"

"Somebody could have called him specifically, on his direct line, whether personal or business. So, if somebody knew him or if somebody might have some pull in that area—like a big donor for the hospital, a rich family on the board, or somebody who's been a director, somebody who hobnobs with these donors—then Dr. Charles might come in response to their call and talk to them in person. However, generally it would be another surgeon or another doctor or even someone in management who would make those kinds of personal contacts, especially for someone who appears without an appointment."

"So, Dr. Charles is a well-placed doctor. Is that what you're saying?"

"Yes, he's the head of the surgical department," she shared. "Sometimes he will come to the ER, so maybe this is just more because of Mason."

"And yet some random guy shouldn't ask questions of Dr. Charles regarding Mason," Jasper pointed out.

"I know, that's why I'm wondering about this discussion caught on tape here. Maybe this is just some guy … getting information, with the surgeon fobbing him off or not checking close enough to see if he has the right to that personal information," she suggested. "It just hit me that it's off."

He studied her for a long moment, then looked back at the video stilled on her phone, now bringing out his own phone. "Let me make some phone calls about that."

She looked over at him. "I don't want to get Dr. Charles in trouble. He's nice. He found me in the parking lot after I got hit by that car."

"So, is he a little distracted? Is he one of those genius people who lives in his head?"

"He's one of those genius people who lives in his heart," she replied, "and he would go the extra mile to help somebody. Thus, if somebody at the hospital was waiting for information, he would normally not be there to interact with the family or the patients. However, if he was, it's quite possible he got stopped and was asked about a patient."

"Interesting. I'll make a quick call."

"To him?" she asked in astonishment.

He nodded. "Yes. Any reason not to?"

She thought about it and shrugged. "I guess not. I'm just not used to the idea of cold-calling somebody like that."

"He'll have to be contacted at some point in time because, if he had any information to give, and he gave it to the now-dead guy, then we need to know about that conversation."

"Right." She frowned.

"Don't worry about it," he said. "I won't get Dr. Charles in trouble."

She flushed. "I would appreciate it if you didn't because he is a good doctor. I wouldn't want to think that he would pay for something I pointed out."

"I'm not the bad guy here, and I'm not getting everybody in trouble. You know that, right?"

"I think you can do it without trying," she muttered. "You just have that knack." His eyebrows shot up, and she nodded. "I think it's complete BS that you're acting as if you aren't the head of this investigation."

"I haven't officially been given that status yet," he stated coolly.

She eyed him intently. "You may not have been given it, but I also think a part of you hasn't formally reached out and taken it, even though in reality you already have it." Surprised, he just stared at her, and she nodded. "You know I do see people, inside and out," she murmured, "so it's not as if this is a surprise to me. You are a hands-on leader, and I don't know whether the other investigators are willing to step into alignment over all this, but it's obvious to me that this is where you belong."

"Now you sound like Tesla," he muttered.

"Whatever pain, problem, or headache happened in your world that sent you away from this work," Amber began, "it's too bad because you're obviously very gifted."

"I haven't done anything yet," he said, looking at her. "You can hardly call me gifted when, so far, all we've done is get your apartment burned."

She started to laugh. "You're right. I hadn't thought about it from that point of view." He shot her a look but they both got up, headed downstairs before moving into the kitchen. She wasn't sure whether he was looking for privacy to make phone calls or what, but, in his house, she did feel like an interloper in some ways, even though he'd made her feel incredibly welcome, cozy and snug, and definitely secure. Whether that was a false sense of security or not, she didn't know.

When he walked back out of the kitchen a few minutes later, he was frowning.

"*Uh-oh.* What's up?"

He shrugged. "He's not on shift at the hospital. So I sent

some people to Dr. Charles's house to speak with him."

She winced. "I don't want to get him in trouble," she reiterated.

"He's not answering his phone," he shared, staring at her intently.

She stared at him for a moment, before she realized what he was saying. "Oh my God." She bolted to her feet, then grabbed her leg and cried out in agony. He swept her into his arms and just held her while she shuddered and shook, catching her breath.

"Remember about looking after yourself," he muttered.

She took several deep breaths and nodded. "I'm working on it. I am, honest."

"Work harder. We can't have you hurting yourself even worse," he stated in a firm tone. "Now we don't know that anything is wrong with the doctor, but we must find him and confirm that he's okay. Then we'll find out what the dead man may have said to him."

"Dr. Charles knows me," she said. "He would talk to me."

"He'll talk to me too," he declared, with a note of amusement in his tone. "He won't have any choice."

"Back to that whole investigator role? You should know that projecting your role as sitting on the sidelines doesn't work when you say things like that," she pointed out.

"Maybe not," he conceded, "but it is very much the way I'm working this right now."

"Right, you're doing what you can do for the moment. Then, after that point in time, you'll change it."

He gave her a smirk and slowly helped her back onto the couch.

"I do need to watch those sudden reactions," she admitted.

"You sure do. The last thing I want is for you to reinjure yourself."

"That's just because you don't want a house guest for too long," she teased, interjecting some levity.

"As far as I'm concerned, … you're here for a couple months. It'll take that long to get your insurance claim through and your new apartment sorted."

She sat in shock, but just then his phone rang.

He stepped back and answered it, his tone turning cool. She settled back to wait for whatever news had developed, but her mind was still stuck on the fact that he considered her being here for more than just a couple days. It certainly added a level of security that she hadn't realized she was looking for. She seemed numb from everything that had happened, with all the constant changes, as new information kept coming in.

She hadn't had a chance to get her balance and to get comfortable in her current situation. Everything was moving too quickly. Yet just knowing that he wasn't expecting her to get out within a day or two was a huge gift and one that she was damn grateful for. At least with that level of stress off her shoulders, she settled back to wait for his return.

Just as she started to relax, her phone rang. As she answered it, she winced because something told her that maybe she should have let it go to voice mail, but too late. "Hello," she answered cautiously.

"Like your present, bitch?" And then the man went off in a horrific round of laughter, and he hung up.

JASPER WALKED BACK into the living room, glad that he at least had some news to tell her, and then he saw the look on her face. "What's the matter?" he asked, racing toward her.

She took a deep breath. "I made the mistake of answering a call on my phone," she said frantically.

"What did they say?" Jasper asked.

"They said, 'Like your present, bitch?'"

He took the phone from her numb fingers and jotted down the last phone number. "It's not blocked," he murmured, "so it'll be an unregistered number." She frowned, almost in disbelief. He shook his head. "Not your problem. Don't you worry about it."

"That's a good thing because I have no idea what I would even do with that information."

He quickly sent off the phone number to be tracked but expected it to likely be a dead end or somebody else's phone or something else.

He got a return call within minutes. "That was Dr. Charles's phone number at his home," Evan declared, with a snap in his tone.

Jasper shook his head. "I just heard from the two officers who went to his house. They stated he was fine, and he would be willing to answer a few questions."

"I don't like the sound of that at all," Evan replied, "but I'm tied up at the hospital."

"Not a problem. I've got somebody else I can send." He quickly hung up and phoned Masters. "I haven't had a reason to pull you further into this, but I could sure use you now."

"What do you need?" Masters asked easily.

Jasper explained the situation about the doctor and the phone call that just came through from his home phone.

"Ah, shit, so you think he's a hostage?"

"I don't know, but check it out, then give me a heads-up as to what we're looking at or if he's got somebody hiding in his house?"

"Which we won't know because, the minute I go up to the front door to check on him—"

"I know. I need a backup plan, but I don't want to move Amber, who's already been attacked. You also don't know the update on what already has happened." Jasper quickly explained about the body dumped outside his home.

When the whistle came through the phone, Masters added, "You've got shit happening, don't you?"

"I do," Jasper confirmed, with a light chuckle.

"What about the rest of your investigators?"

"I haven't been able to reach Sam, and Morgan is at the morgue right now with our most recent dead body. I don't want to send him on a wild goose chase if that's what this is. Not sure about Lichen. I think the other guys mentioned Lichen was due for three weeks of leave. As far as I'm concerned, better he's gone right now."

"I don't think anything is a wild goose chase," Masters noted casually, "and I'm already on my way over to the doc's place."

"Good enough. I'm hoping it's nothing, but—"

"Yeah, I'll give you a report in about twenty minutes," Masters said, before he disconnected.

As Jasper turned, Amber was staring at him.

"What was that?" she asked.

"The phone number your caller used returned as Dr. Charles's home office."

She stared at him. "So, that's even more reason to be worried."

"Yet it shouldn't be because I had confirmation from two officers that they had just spoken to him at the front door, and everything appeared to be fine."

"Then this guy called." She shook her phone and stared at Jasper.

"I know," he replied, putting a hand on hers to calm her down. "I know. So, now I have somebody else heading over there to see what the true situation is."

She swallowed. "Dr. Charles is a good man."

"I'm glad to hear that, and we'll find out very soon, so not to worry."

"Finding out is one thing," she noted, "but finding out before something ugly happens is a whole different story."

"We'll get there."

"I know Dr. Charles. I know him quite well," she repeated, as she looked around. "Take me to his house to speak with him."

"What good would that do?" Jasper asked.

"I don't know. Yet I feel l should be there for him." Just then her phone rang again. She stared down at the number and whispered, "I think this is the same number." He looked at it and nodded, urging her to answer it again. She leaned in close to Jasper, so he could hear their conversation. "What do you want?" she cried out.

"I want to take out a couple birds with one stone," he replied. "So I could use you over at the good doctor's place, and it would be a lie to say he is fine. The man is not doing very well at all. In fact, he might need some medical attention." In the background, she heard some moaning.

She twisted to look up at Jasper in horror. "I'm on my way. Of course I would be a lot more mobile if you hadn't tried to run me down."

An ugly silence came on the other end of the phone. "You're too damn smart for your own good, bitch. You know that, right? Get over here in the next ten minutes, or I'll pop this guy, and, this time, nobody'll fix him." And, with that, he hung up.

"You're not going anywhere," Jasper growled, his tone firm as he glared at her. His mind was already racing to figure out how to get her to stay here and maybe have a policewoman fill in.

She shook her head. "None of the conniving going around in your brain right now will work," she declared. "We're on the clock. We only have ten minutes to get there, less than ten minutes now. I won't leave Dr. Charles in his hour of need." She was already heading to the front door. "You can either take me and maybe it will help, or maybe it won't. Or you can stay here and run things from the background." He swore out loud, and she shrugged. "I could just sit around here too, but I would much rather get to work."

He gave a bitter laugh. "You know how this will end."

"It'll end with us capturing this asshole," she stated, "and then maybe we can focus on getting Mason's shooter taken care of. That's what this is all about. So, yes, we must do whatever we need to in order to make this happen, but let's do everything we can to deal with Dr. Charles, with what we've got in front of us too."

He shook his head. "I don't like the idea of your leaving Fort Knox."

"Fort Knox is great if you live in it forever," she pointed out, with a clipped nod. "But the reality is, we live in this world. And it just called me out of Fort Knox. So, one way or another, I will answer that call."

AMBER KNEW SHE'D upset Jasper, but nothing else could be done. She would not sit back and let a good man die because she hadn't been willing to step outside. She was the one who had started this by taking a video of the now-dead man talking to Dr. Charles, so she would have to be the one who dealt with it. As she made her way to the garage, she realized she didn't have any wheels. Closing her eyes, she stiffened her spine, then turned and said, "Please, Jasper." She could almost see the wheels turning in the back of his head.

He finally nodded. "Let's go." He led her to his vehicle. He helped her into the passenger seat, then walked around to the driver's side. "Just for the record," he stated, as he got in, slamming the door a little harder than necessary, "I don't agree with this."

"Objection duly noted," she murmured. "And, just for the record, it doesn't change anything. He's a good doctor, and I couldn't live with myself if I hadn't done what I could to try and help right now."

He shook his head. "We don't even know if he's still alive."

"No, we don't," she admitted, "but, if he is, … I am a nurse and know what to do to try and help him. On the other hand, if this guy sees you, he's likely to shoot you right between the eyes, and you'll be of no help to anyone."

He shook his head. "And he won't do that to you?"

She frowned, then shrugged. "It's a possibility. I get that. I don't want to think about it, but I'm not stupid either. It's possible."

"It's not only possible, it's quite likely that his intention is to eliminate anybody who had contact with the man from the ER, our dead John Doe," he stated. "And that includes you."

"Yes, but maybe, if I can check on the doctor, … maybe I can find a way to extend this long enough for you to take him out," she suggested. "You'll have to be smart about it, or he'll take one look at you and shoot first, ask questions later. I'm an ER nurse. I know all too well that people don't keep walking when they've got bullet holes in their brain."

He gave her a faint smile. "You're right. They usually don't," he agreed, "but the gunman will still have to hit me first, and I don't kill easily." And, with that, he drove to the doctor's home, done in silence, at least on her part. Jasper, on the other hand, barked out a steady stream of orders to various people over the phone, while driving fast to meet their deadline.

As soon as they got to the doctor's house, she looked at it and sighed. "Did you have to park in full view?"

"Absolutely. I'm done hiding from this asshole. So whatever he's got to say, whatever it is he thinks he'll do, he needs to do it."

"You realize that'll mean a bullet hole, right? He'll take one look at you and start shooting."

"We've already discussed that point, but, in a very short order, he'll decide that you're trouble, and he'll take you out too."

Amber shuddered at the possibility. "Let's go see if we can both avoid getting shot, help Dr. Charles, and get this done."

With that, Jasper shut off the engine, hopped out, and came around to her side, where he opened the door.

"You could have just let me out," she noted. "You could literally just let me walk to the door, and he wouldn't know that you are anything other than a ride."

"He's undoubtedly already expecting me too, for no other reason than he dropped the dead guy outside my house, probably knowing that ahead of time."

She winced, realizing he was right.

"Let's go," Jasper stated.

"Is it just the two of us?"

"No, I already contacted Masters, and he's on his way too."

"And yet he's not part of the original team."

He gave her a flat look, then smiled ferociously. "Now how do you know that?"

"What? I don't know this? I can't know this?"

"How do you know I didn't get to bring in a few men on this case?"

She sighed. "If you weren't so damn secretive, people would have a much better idea about how you guys operate."

"They might. Absolutely they might," he agreed, "but being secretive is what has kept me alive this far, so I'm not likely to change it now." He wrapped an arm around her shoulders, as they walked up to the door. "Come on. Let's go face the music, even if it's the funeral march."

TESLA STARED AT Markus in shock. "They did what?" she asked, her voice rising to a high-pitched squeak.

Markus nodded, his face grim. "Yeah, and that's where we're at right now, still waiting for an update."

She looked over at Mason, then back at Markus. "Good God, what is going on?"

"That's what we'll sort out, and we don't have any idea

whether the doctor is alive or dead."

"But he performed a miracle to keep Mason alive," she whispered, her heart breaking. "It's not fair that somebody would target him, not for doing a brilliant job."

"Maybe too brilliant, as far as these people are concerned. If assassination of Mason was the end goal, nobody will be happy with the surgeon who pulled out all the stops to keep Mason alive."

She nodded but found it hard to imagine that somebody would willfully do such a thing. "So, they're going in?" she asked, feeling faint at the thought.

"Yes," he confirmed, his tone grim. "We do have a team moving into place around the house, but …"

"But what?" she asked.

Markus sighed. "The nurse, Amber, is involved, just because she is kind and is worried about the doctor. Then the doctor is involved, literally because he was doing his job and did a phenomenal job saving Mason. And now … Jasper is there too."

Tesla closed her eyes at that thought. She could not bear the thought of losing Jasper. They'd become so close over the years. He was more like a brother than a cousin to her. Maybe a brother she had lost a long time ago, but Jasper had been there for her, and she couldn't bear not being there for him now.

She opened her eyes, her resolve returning, as she squared her shoulders and gave Markus a hard look. "What can I do?"

He shook his head. "You? Nothing." She frowned at him, and he smiled. "The warrior is on it," he stated.

"But *the warrior*," she replied, her eyebrow arched, "hasn't solved it yet. There are moving pieces still, so what can I do?"

He hesitated. "You looked at all the relevant videos. We've ID'd the dead guy, some local gun for hire," he began. "Amber pointed out Dr. Charles partially in the video, talking with our dead guy. So we are now working hard to figure out who else is involved, whether with the Amber angle and her video or directly with Mason. The general attitude is that the two must be connected, simply by that video she took. It's too bizarre to have two major issues like this and not find a link."

She tilted her head. "I would agree with that. … I can start running down more of this information. I was doing some of it, though not very much. I didn't have access to the details I needed and never got set up the way I should have. I intended to discuss it with Jasper and never should have let up on that."

"Let up on what?" Markus asked in astonishment. "It wasn't your job. We were just to keep you calm and the baby safe."

"The baby is safe," Tesla declared in a determined tone. "Never doubt that."

"Oh, I don't doubt it," he said, with a wry look in her direction. "That doesn't mean we need Mom running around and getting stressed out herself."

She smiled. "This baby is part of me. She'll be tough, just like me."

"She?" he asked, with an eyebrow raised.

"Feels like a she," she admitted. "I hope it's a she." She glanced back over at Mason. "Mason hopes it's a girl too, but, as long as it's a healthy baby, it won't matter. Even if it's not healthy, obviously our hearts would break for anything other than the perfectly healthy child we're hoping for, but we will love him or her, no matter what."

He nodded. "I wouldn't expect anything else."

"So keep me busy, so I'm not dwelling on the negatives here."

Markus sighed. "If you want to run the data we've gathered so far—looking for crossovers, for connections, for other known allies—you could do that. Nobody can analyze data better than you."

"I'm on it," she replied, as she looked around and frowned at him. "Can you get me set up with a small table?"

"For?"

"I can't use a lap table effectively," she noted, patting her large belly with a smile. "And an office chair. I want it set up in the corner over here. I've got my laptop, and I will get on this." She determinedly got up and started moving her bags around the floor.

"Wait," he muttered, holding up a hand.

"No, go now."

He hesitated, but she shook her head. "Not the time to argue, Markus. Even when I do get information for you, there is no guarantee it will be helpful or even timely. All I can do is start cross-referencing data to find who all might have been able and available to do something about this, and who might want to," she explained. "Everything else is more or less intangible."

He took a moment, then nodded. "Fine. I'll get you set up, but I need you to take care of yourself."

"I will. I promise. If Mason wakes up, he'll need—"

"*If* Mason wakes up?"

"No." She shook her head. "*When* Mason wakes up, he will need me, but, in the meantime, we must get whoever it is who's intent on killing him." She looked up to see Evan step inside, sighing at the sight of her moving her cot. She rolled her eyes. "Don't tell me that you've been dragged into this again too."

"No," he countered, one eyebrow raised. "It's our honor to be here and to be a part of this."

Instantly she felt tears gathering in the back of her eyes, and she nodded. "I'm sorry. I'm just a little stressed."

His boyish grin flashed. "I would expect nothing else, considering the stressful situation you're in," he noted, with a nod. "We're on it. Though it might not look as if we're getting very far, we are making progress."

"I'll help more too," she murmured, "by setting up a proper workstation." She then looked over at Markus. "Why are you still here?"

CHAPTER 14

AMBER TIGHTLY GRIPPED Jasper's hand, as they slowly made their way to the front door. She took a deep breath and asked, "Why does it feel like I'm walking into a death trap?"

"Probably because you are," he stated calmly. "We can leave anytime."

From the inside, she heard a moan, and she winced. "No, I can't." Not giving herself a chance to change her mind, she rapped hard on the door.

"Come in."

She looked over at Jasper, then pushed open the door and stepped inside, Jasper still holding her hand to support her, as he stepped forward with her.

"You were told to come alone," the man said, from somewhere in the darkness.

"No, you didn't tell me to do that," she argued. "You didn't say anything about that."

After a short pause came a half laugh. "Pretty cocky for somebody who's facing down a gun."

"Not the first time," she murmured.

He stepped out of the shadows, and Amber saw a man she didn't recognize. She didn't know anything about him, and she frowned. "Why on earth do you want to kill me and this lovely doctor?"

"Because this *lovely doctor* did such a damn good job, and he saved somebody who wasn't supposed to be saved."

"Mason," she stated, with a nod. "You think the entire base isn't looking for you?"

"That's nice. Do I look like I care?" With a brutal laugh, he glared at Jasper beside her. "What the hell do you want, tough guy?"

"Nothing," Jasper replied. "I came here with her."

"Her bodyguard?"

"Her partner," he stated coolly. "Nobody takes what's mine."

She stiffened under the possessive tone of his voice and wasn't sure whether he was acting or something else was to this bravado. It's not that she was angered by it by any means. If anything, that protectiveness was lovely to hear, especially right now. Jasper squeezed her fingers, and she responded by gripping his even harder. If nothing else he was a lifeline for her right now, one that she desperately needed.

"What have you done with the good doctor?" Jasper asked.

The gunman shrugged. "Gave him a taste of his own medicine."

She didn't even want to comprehend what that meant for a man who did surgeries on the worst and hardest cases. "Let me see him," she stated abruptly.

He laughed. "Why? Do you think you'll save him?"

"Maybe, if you left me anything to save."

"I was hoping not to, but he's tougher than I imagined."

She winced. "Then let me look at him."

"I guess if you keep him alive, I can just beat him up

some more," he added, grinning at her.

The darkness in his soul was hard to ignore. "That's what you do? You just beat people up?"

"Sure, why not?" he murmured, with a casual wave of his hand. "You can go in and see him, but your buddy here cannot." She stiffened because she knew exactly what reaction that would bring about from Jasper, and she wasn't wrong.

"In that case she's not going anywhere," Jasper declared, hanging on to her arm tightly.

She looked over at him. "I have to go see Dr. Charles."

"No, you don't," he argued, "not unless this guy will give you free rein to go in and to come back out again."

"She's the one who came here, so obviously she cares more about the doctor than you do."

"I don't think so," Jasper countered, "but somehow you managed to make her feel guilty about this whole thing."

"And so she should. If she hadn't taken that damn video, we wouldn't be here right now."

"That's like saying, if you hadn't come to the hospital with ill intent to figure out whether your shot went wrong or not," she declared in a hard tone, "we wouldn't be here either."

She heard Jasper moan under his breath at her tone, but she was past caring. If she would die here, she would die here, but she would be damned if she would die muzzled. "I don't know why you felt it necessary to try and kill Mason. He's well loved by everybody," she cried out.

"Not everybody," the gunman corrected, glaring at her, "and you don't know anything."

"I don't know anything," she repeated, with a shriek of frustration, "because you won't tell me anything."

He nodded. "You're damn right. I won't. This guy let himself get caught, and that is why he's dead."

She frowned. "You don't mean *this guy* as in *the doctor*?"

"No, not him, but …" Then their gunman stopped and frowned.

"Right, the friend you left as *a gift*."

"Did you like that?" he asked, with an odd excitement.

"Not particularly. I like my men alive, not dead."

He burst out laughing, thinking that was some hilarious joke.

It wasn't. She was dead serious, but there would be no talking to this guy.

"Pretty damn cheeky for somebody in your position," the gunman snarled.

She shrugged. "Then shoot me now," she dared him. "I don't even know why you wanted to bring me here."

"I want the video."

She frowned at him. "What difference does it make? You've already killed the guy in the video. He's dead. The police have his body, so what freaking difference does it make now?"

He repeated, "I want the video."

She shrugged, pulled out her phone, and tossed it at him. "It's there."

He tossed it back at her. "Bring it up. Let me see it."

She unlocked her phone and brought up the video, then tossed it back at him. He hit Play and studied the video. Then, as if realizing nothing here made a difference, he smiled. "Good, this is nice and clean then."

"Nothing's nice and clean about leaving bodies everywhere," Jasper declared, his tone hard.

"There'll be a couple more now," the gunman threatened. "You shouldn't have come with your girlfriend."

"Maybe I shouldn't have, but she was insistent about coming to see the doctor. Dr. Charles has been a friend."

"That's her fault. She should never have signed up for something like that," the gunman stated. "What an idiot boyfriend you are to let her do this."

"*Let* me do this?" she asked in a hard tone.

He rolled his eyes. "What are you, some feminist? She's not worth it, you know," the gunman added abruptly, addressing Jasper.

Jasper smiled and stated, "Yes, she is."

The gunman snorted at that. "Man, you've got it bad."

"Maybe," Jasper said cheerfully, "but it's not your problem."

"No, it isn't because you'll both die now," he snapped, glaring at her. "You didn't expect to get away from here, did you?"

"Maybe not, but we want to see that Dr. Charles was okay."

"He's not doing okay," the gunman stressed in exasperation. "I never intended for him to be okay."

She stared at him steadily. "And yet you haven't killed him, but you could have."

"No, I needed him to bring you in."

She shrugged. "I'm here. Now what?"

And, with that, the tableau froze. The gunman glared at her. "I'm not sure what I'll do about you, but the doctor will die, and your little pet here will also die."

She frowned at the gunman. "You'll seriously call him a pet? Wow." She looked over at Jasper. "I think you just got demoted."

He shrugged, his gaze never leaving the gunman. "Maybe." He gripped her hand tighter and lifted his free hand to his head and scratched. "And maybe not."

The gunman lifted his gun arm, pointed it at him, and asked, "Any last words?"

A red dot appeared on the gunman's forehead.

"Yeah," Jasper replied, with half a smile. "Die, mother-fucker." Then he dropped his raised hand. Almost instantly glass shattered all around them, and now a dripping red dot appeared on the gunman's forehead, as he and his gun fell harmlessly to the ground.

Amber was frozen, as it all seemed to happen so fast. She was too stunned to even think. Thankfully she didn't react and hurt herself further.

Jasper released her hand and muttered, "Go on, honey. Take a look at the doctor and see how bad he is. I'm calling an ambulance." She took another look at their gunman, then headed in the direction of the moans. There on the floor was Dr. Charles, bloody, puffy, and bruised, one eye openly staring at her in horror.

She eased herself down beside him, grasped his hand, and whispered, "It's all right. It's over. You're safe now."

He closed his eyes and whispered, "Thank God."

"Let me check you over," she murmured.

"Spleen," he whispered. "I think he ruptured my spleen."

"Well, good, that's something we can fix," she replied, trying for a cheerful tone.

"I could," he said, "but I'm not so sure about my residents."

She chuckled, relieved to hear the humor in his voice. "You keep that sense of humor. You know perfectly well we have some very talented people on staff."

"I know," he whispered, "but, damn, I'm tired."

"I don't want you going out now," she warned him, and he opened his eyes. "Remember how I need you awake. You know the drill, Doctor. I need you conscious, and we have an ambulance on the way."

"And if I can't stay awake?" he asked, that same thread of amusement in his voice.

"In that case, I'll have to throw ice water in your face. And I'm not sure whether that will hurt you or help you, considering your face has already been beaten up."

"You've probably just been waiting for a chance to do that," he teased, trying for a smile that looked horrible on him, "but I'm damn glad to see you."

"I'm damn glad to see you alive," she muttered. "I was afraid you were a goner."

"He kept threatening me, telling me that he had one more thread to tie up, and then I would be history," he shared. "I don't even know what I did."

"You saved Mason," she replied, "although I'm not sure whether or not he shot Mason."

"It wasn't him," Dr. Charles stated. "He told me something about he was a scout, sent to the hospital to keep an eye on everything, and it all went to hell, when I fixed up somebody I shouldn't have."

"Yeah," she said calmly, "and, if this guy isn't the sniper who fired the shot, then we're still looking for somebody else."

"He made it seem that he was part of a team."

She thought about that, as she checked him over. Her left hand applied pressure on the wound bleeding the worst. "Looks like he broke an arm, and your ankle is in rough shape, and well …" She stopped and winced. "That gorgeous face of yours appears to have a broken nose."

He snorted. "That'll be like the twelfth time," he pointed out. "I don't think it'll fix anymore."

"Don't worry. The girls will still love you anyway."

He gave her a sad smile. "Lost my wife a long time ago," he murmured, sounding like a lost puppy. "I haven't been in the market since."

"No, but maybe you should reconsider that now," she suggested. "You've been given a second chance to live. Maybe it's time to find somebody to share it with."

He then came back with another one-liner that had her chuckling. "I can't. You already came in with somebody, didn't you?"

She nodded. "Yeah, apparently I ended up with a guardian angel."

"Good," he said, "but see what I mean? All the good ones are taken." Then he groaned softly and whispered, "I don't think I can stay conscious."

"What is it we're always telling our patients?" she murmured, and his eyes opened wide, as he stared at her through the puffiness. She nodded. "It's not an option. You stay awake, and you do not give up on me."

"I'm not giving up," he whispered, "but I feel pretty rough."

"I know you do," she acknowledged, sympathy in her tone, but she couldn't let him succumb to that pain. "The ambulance will be here momentarily."

"*Momentarily* doesn't sound quite the same when it's your version of the word."

She smiled down at him, stroking the hair off his bruised and bloodied face with her free hand. "Just think," she added. "You're a hero."

"No, I'm so not a hero. I didn't do anything. As a matter of fact, I begged him to let me go."

"And you feel bad about that?" she asked in astonishment. "I would have begged right off the bat," she noted, with a chuckle. "You can't feel bad about anything to do with these people. They're assholes, and we are the good people. We spend our lives saving people, and sometimes, when we get on the wrong side of humanity, it can be ugly because we don't have the tools to deal with the assholes. You did just fine."

"Ah, I don't know about that."

"Don't ever feel ashamed of begging for your life," she stated. "Every man, every woman would do exactly the same thing, if they found themselves in the same situation."

He let out a gentle sigh. "I think you're wrong, but you make me feel better, and, for the moment, I'll let you."

She chuckled. "And that's a good thing. You *should* let me because you've done good today." In the distance, she heard sirens, and she smiled. "Hear that? … The sirens are almost here."

"You're just telling me that so I don't fall asleep," he murmured.

"You should hear them yourself," she stated. "Open your eyes. Look at me. Look at me."

Under duress, he opened his good eye and stared up at her.

She nodded. "Now listen. Then tell me that you can hear them." In the distance, the sirens were getting louder and louder.

The relief was easy to see in his gaze, as he whispered, "Thank God."

"I know, but it is happening, and you'll be okay. Just

hold tight." After that, things happened at a pace that she knew to expect, and yet it still seemed almost in slow motion, as she watched and waited for the team to come in.

She gave them the little bit of information that she had for them, and they quickly packed up the doctor and moved him out into the ambulance and away.

As she stood up and stepped outside, she looked around at the strange light and realized that they were lights from what looked like one million vehicles parked outside. Blinded, she stumbled out the front door and was caught from behind and wrapped up in strong, warm arms. Instinctively she knew who held her, and she buried her face against Jasper's chest, choking back the sobs that she wanted to let loose but didn't dare quite yet.

"It's all right," he whispered, as he held her close. "I'll get you home soon. Then you can crash."

She looked up at him. "Keep telling me that, and I might believe you. All I could do was keep Dr. Charles focused, keep him awake, and keep pressure on some of that bleeding."

"That's what he will remember." Jasper hesitated and then asked, "He will remember, right?"

"I think so," she said. "He thought his spleen was ruptured, which is the most worrisome. He has multiple injuries, but the rest are more incapacitating, rather than life-threatening—a broken nose and broken arm, maybe a bruised ankle. I don't understand how people can do things like that."

"That's a very strategic tactic," Jasper noted calmly. "Incapacitate them so they can't come after you, and then you continue to toy and torment them."

"Toying and tormenting a good man like that?" she

asked, staring up at him. "Did I ever tell you that I don't like people?"

"I'm pretty sure that, even if you haven't told me, I would still understand," he replied, with a gentle smile.

She relaxed a bit and looked around. When someone called out, she stiffened, and he just held her close. When people approached, she lifted her head, looked around, and saw the police, plus several men she didn't recognize, but they were all talking to Jasper. She listened as the conversation rippled around her for a few moments. Then she was asked to provide whatever additional information she had. When someone specifically asked if the doctor had told her anything, she nodded.

"He did," she whispered and then proceeded to tell them the little bits and pieces he had shared.

"Shit, this gunman was part of a whole team?"

"Something like that," she murmured, "though I'm not exactly sure what a team looks like in a case like this."

"Neither do we," Jasper admitted, with a nod, "but we'll find out." He looked at the guys all around him.

A few she thought she recognized and thought maybe a couple were the ones Jasper had been working with, but she wasn't sure.

"I'm taking her home. She's still in rough shape from the hit-and-run," Jasper explained. "So, if you want to meet at my place, that's fine. I just need to get her off her feet."

She groaned. "I'm fine. I can hold up a bit longer."

Looking at her, he shook his head. "Nope, that will just make you worse off in the long run. No point in saving one person at the expense of another. I told you that already."

"As I recall, it seemed to be more of an order at the time. I don't recall there being a whole lot of discussion about it."

He chuckled. "Not my fault you didn't listen," he quipped, as he unreservedly moved her toward his vehicle.

She sighed with relief. "I am tired."

"Let's go. Let's get you home."

She collapsed into the seat, feeling a weariness like she hadn't experienced in a very long time.

He looked over at her, as he started the engine. "Are you okay?"

"I will be," she murmured. "It had a happy ending, after all."

He nodded.

"You could have told me what your plans were," she burst out, "so I wouldn't have been so worried."

"Yeah, and when was I supposed to do that?"

She frowned, realizing that she hadn't given him a whole lot of options for talking. She shrugged. "Maybe I didn't give you a chance. I don't know. I was just keeping the gunman's attention on me, hoping you could figure something out. But I sure would have felt better had I known what to expect."

"But the reality is, that would have changed the way you behaved, so you might have given it away."

She winced. "That's true. I might have."

"You've shown enough bravado already," he stated in a dry tone. When she glared at him, he smiled and nodded. "Come on. You know it yourself."

"I had to get to Dr. Charles," she said, with a nod. "I've seen him save people who were well past the point of saving," she murmured. "He's a truly gifted surgeon, and, even if I was lost, the world needed him."

He looked over at her and grabbed her hand. "The world needs you too," he murmured.

She sat back, closed her eyes, and whispered, "Jasper, let's go home."

JASPER DAMN NEAR had a heart attack, watching Amber arguing with the gunman about going in to see Dr. Charles. The fact that she had done what she did and did it in the way she had done it, made Jasper like her even more. The fact that he already liked her, had already opened his heart to her, was something he was still coming to terms with. Hard not to since she was special in so many ways, but the last thing he wanted right now was a relationship, particularly when he was involved in this case, which had already taken several ugly turns.

They had gotten through this leg of it, and nobody was more grateful than Jasper, but it still could get much uglier so quickly that he didn't want Amber involved in any way. Yet he knew he would have to fight to keep her out of it.

What he had to do was convince her to stay at his house, and, if he was lucky, convince her to stay long enough for them to get to know each other well enough for him to determine whether this attraction he felt was two-way or just one. He wanted to believe it went both ways, but he'd been wrong before. Lessons learned from the past held him back, when there had probably been opportunities he could have taken. However, she was injured anyway. Plus, he wanted time, time to go slowly, time to realize whether this was something serious or the complete opposite.

And it didn't seem they would get a whole lot of time right now either. He had to work. He had to deal with this Mason shooting.

As he pulled into his garage and locked the doors behind them, she asked, "Is the team coming?"

"They'll be here in a few hours. Everybody will do a regroup right now."

"Good enough. Will they consider it rude if I go lie down?"

He chuckled. "They're all expecting you to go lie down and are probably waiting for that, so you're not in the middle of the meeting."

She opened her eyes and asked, "Do I need to be part of it?"

"No, but I'll fill you in afterward."

She looked up at him and smiled. "I think you probably will, if only to ensure that I stay out of trouble."

He nodded, as he opened the passenger door and helped her out. "Be sure you take some painkillers," he suggested, "or you'll be damn sore tomorrow."

"I will," she said. "Did you mean it about staying at your house for the next few days?"

"I said a lot longer than a few days. How about you staying long enough for us to see if we have anything?" At that, she opened her eyes wide and stared at him. "Or will you just pretend absolutely nothing is there?"

"No, I definitely won't pretend that," she replied. "I was just thinking we might have more time to work it out later."

"We might, or we might not."

"Good point," she murmured. "In that case, as long as you're okay with a house guest for a little while, I'll stay."

"I want you to stay at least until all this is put to rest," he confirmed. "I don't know how many other people might know what your involvement was tonight, but I don't want them coming back after you." He watched the color fade from her skin, and he nodded. "So, please consider yourself a most welcome guest."

"No strings?" she asked warily.

"No strings," he declared, his eyes open wide. "Unless you want to tie them."

She stared up at him and asked, "Seriously?"

He shrugged. "At least if we spend some time together, we can see if anything long-term is between us."

"I already feel as if there is. I just don't know that I can trust it."

"You and me both," he admitted. "I think *walking wounded* in terms of relationships might apply, … at least to me."

"To you, yes," she agreed. "I don't have that excuse."

"And you don't need one," he told her, as he led her into the living room and up the stairs. "Remember that you get to be you. You don't have to be anybody else."

She smiled. "As long as you remember that too. You don't have to be anybody else either."

He burst out laughing. "And, of course, you would throw my words at me."

"Of course," she said, "because it's far too easy to get hung up on the rights and the wrongs without being *that* person. Right now, I think we've had a lucky escape, and I, for one, need some rest."

"Go for it," he said. "I'll meet with the guys, and then I will check up on you. However, if you're sleeping, I won't wake you," he promised.

"Good, because I'm not sure I'll even get back to sleep. The nightmares will be something else."

He stared at her and nodded. "Anytime you need to be reassured, you give me a call."

"We'll see, but right now, I'll just sleep." And, with that, she took the last few steps into her bedroom and closed the door.

He stood outside for a long moment, wondering if he should have said something more, but he found it hard to go in that direction right now. When the door opened again, and she stepped back out, he smiled.

"You still haven't left," she noted, returning his smile.

"No, I'm still here, still contemplating life."

She nodded. "Probably more than contemplating life, but I just wanted to give you something else to contemplate." And, with that, she pulled his head down and gave him a big kiss. When she broke away, she smiled at him. "Thank you for saving my life."

And she turned and walked back into the bedroom and shut the door once more.

CHAPTER 15

AMBER LISTENED FOR sounds of the others arriving, but it appeared to be quiet down below. She wasn't sure if she would even hear them, considering this place was as much of a fortress as it was. She had had a hot shower and sat down on the side of the bed, wondering if she was even ready to sleep. She was tired, but that didn't mean that sleep was ready for her. As she stretched out on the bed to relax her leg, her phone rang. Amber checked her Caller ID and then asked, "Tesla, are you okay? Is Mason okay?"

"I'm calling to make sure *you*'re okay," Tesla replied. "I feel terrible that anybody who was helping us or was being kind to us is being targeted."

Amber sighed. "I understand exactly how you feel because that's just what I went through," she murmured. "I feel bad because, if I hadn't taken that video, then, in theory, a lot of this wouldn't have happened."

"Ah, we're always so good at blaming ourselves, aren't we?" asked Tesla.

"I think we're too good at it," Amber noted. "You aren't to blame, and I'm not to blame, and I think that's where we have to leave it."

"I wonder if we can," Tesla murmured. "I'm glad to

know that you survived this horrible evening and that the doctor survived as well."

"I was just about to call the hospital and see if I could get an update on him," Amber shared. "Honestly you need to thank Jasper. He saved my life."

"I'll thank Jasper myself," she noted. "He's very good at what he does. He tends to forget that and doesn't necessarily fill us in on everything he has planned."

"No, … he certainly didn't in my case either," she muttered in disgust. "I walked right into that mess, fully prepared to die in order to have Dr. Charles survive. He is incredibly gifted, and he's done so much for so many people that I just couldn't see that my life had more value than his. Yet, of course, Jasper didn't tell me that he had a plan."

Tesla burst out laughing. "Jasper *always* has a plan," she declared. "Even when you think there's no plan, there's a plan."

"That's encouraging," Amber replied. "I'm still struggling to get a read on him."

"In what way?" Tesla asked, her curiosity highlighted in her tone.

Amber winced, knowing she had given something away already. "He broached the subject that he would like to get to know me better."

After a moment of silence, Tesla murmured, "You, my dear, should feel very blessed. He's an awfully good man, and he will never hurt you or do anything to bring harm to your world. He's been very badly burned."

"He touched on that a little bit," Amber noted, "but I got the impression that he doesn't move quickly or trust easily."

"Let me tell you a little bit about it," she began, "particularly if you like him." Then she stopped and waited.

"I do like him," Amber confirmed. "I don't want gratitude to be mixed up in this, and I would love a chance to get to know him more, but there's this hesitation because I don't understand where the block is, but there definitely is one."

"Oh, there definitely is one," Tesla noted, "so let me explain. … It started a few years back, when he was involved in a pretty in-depth case. He's done a lot of internal affairs work. He had met somebody with whom he fell head over heels in love. They got engaged because she was perfect, absolutely everything he ever wanted. At the time, … he was so happy, and it was so lovely to see him so happy. Yet I didn't like her at all, and I didn't know how I was supposed to reconcile things with my cousin, who I adored, and his woman, who he adored and I just couldn't tolerate. I didn't know what to say to him. Meanwhile, I tried so hard to be friendly to her, and yet something kept holding me back."

"What happened?"

"To make a long story short, by the end of the day, he was engaged, in love, and ready to quit his job and build an entire life with her—until he found out that the people he was bringing down on his current case were people she was working with. Her brother was heavily involved, and she had only gotten involved with Jasper in order to protect her brother. So she intended to calm down Jasper and to get him to drop the case or potentially not even survive with his own life. He was definitely not meant to survive within his career or to continue working on any cases involving her brother. Jasper was a patsy, after being set up and used by her. I don't think he's trusted himself ever since, and he hasn't trusted his own judgment, and he certainly hasn't trusted any women," Tesla noted.

"Oh my God," Amber murmured. "He did say something about it but much more cryptically than that, so I didn't realize it was quite so horrific."

"It was, and it's been hard for him ever since. It nearly broke him. He's a good man. He's more than a good man," she stated, "but, when you take a beating like that on so many levels, you don't know who is trustworthy anymore. More than that, you don't know if you can trust yourself. I think that was the hardest thing for him, realizing that his own judgment had failed him."

"And yet it hadn't," Amber argued. "That woman wasn't for real. He fell in love with a mirage, but it was almost impossible for him to know it."

"Of course," Tesla agreed. "So, it might be a bit of work to get to the point where he can trust you or to where he's prepared to make that step. He will need some time. He'll need some distance, and, if you are so lucky as to have him be a part of your heart, he will be loyal forever. He'll never cheat, and he'll never hurt you willingly, and he will go the distance to always ensure that you're taken care of," she added. "And, if he even intimated that he wanted to get to know you better, you're the luckiest woman in the world. Well, … except for me, of course."

"Except for you," Amber confirmed, with a half a laugh, "because you have Mason."

"Yes," she agreed, her laughter coming through the phone. "Jasper's a good man, but he'll move very slowly, and then …" She stopped. "Unless you don't want him to move at that pace."

"Meaning?"

"Meaning that sometimes we have to take a bit more control over the pace of our relationships," she shared, with a chuckle, "but only if you're ready, only if that is something you want to do."

"I think I understand what you mean."

"Of course you do. You're a smart lady. According to him, you're also fearless, loyal, brave, and he likes you."

She stared at the phone in delight. "He told you that?"

"He did, and he knows perfectly well what he has in front of him too," she said. "It sounds to me as if you two are made for each other."

"I don't know about that," Amber murmured. "It's so soon. Yet I could hope for something like that. It's just … not always that easy to trust."

"Of course it's very hard to trust, … but one of you has to open their heart first, to see if something is there."

"I have feelings for him. Yet my brain is telling me how it's pretty early yet," she explained. "However, he did say something about taking some time to get to know each other."

"Sure, but that's not a brush-off, more like him parking you, for an uncertain date in time when he will be prepared to open that door and to step through it. Are you ready to wait for that? Even if it takes months?"

Amber snorted. "Yeah, I can see how it could be *months* because he won't jump into this lightly."

"But you have time, and you can think about it, and, when you're ready to decide, you may just have to take matters into your own hands."

"Thanks for the heads-up," Amber murmured, as she ended the call. She was wet from her shower and still not dressed, but she quickly put on her nightshirt, grateful beyond belief that they had packed most of her clothes when Jasper had suddenly decided they must move to his place— right before her apartment was burned down, along with everything she had left behind. Thankfully she wasn't a keeper of stuff, and Jasper had encouraged her to bring anything important, so no one would get their hands on it in her absence.

As she thought about him and the olive branch he had extended and how he had taken care of her and her life, had saved her several times, she realized so much more was between them. Was she prepared to wait, or would she grab all that bravado she had shown earlier today and do something about it, way ahead of his schedule?

She thought long and hard about it, and, when she heard noises downstairs and then finally footsteps coming upstairs, she knew she must make a decision.

WITH EVERYBODY'S NOTES collated, Jasper sent them all on their way. He needed to sleep too, and the good news was that the doctor would make it and was out of surgery right now. Jasper wondered if he should stop in and tell Amber the results of his update on the doctor. That was probably asking for trouble, and that was something he would avoid at all costs.

He headed to his room and stepped under a hot spray of water, as he eased back the tension and the stress from his day. Seeing her arguing with the gunman had defied belief, yet he understood why she'd done it. It made him admire her even more, but it could have quickly turned bad. Somebody like him, with the experience he had, understood that she had the bravado, the courage of the innocent, and it had served her well in this instance, but it may not ever again.

He knew that he would have nightmares for days to

come, reliving her actions and how she had completely disregarded her own life and the value of it in order to save the doctor's life. Admirable, yet not so admirable. It also meant that she didn't see that *she* had so much more to give. He understood why she'd done what she'd done, but it was still frustrating to see her risk her life for another.

When he stepped out of the shower, he shaved, got ready for bed, and then, with a towel wrapped around his waist, stepped into his room and froze. She sat on his bed, obviously waiting for him. He raised one eyebrow. "Amber?"

She looked up and smiled. "Jasper."

"Are you all right? How's the leg?"

"I'm fine, and the leg's fine."

He didn't understand something in her tone. He stared at her warily.

She nodded. "Yeah, I'm probably a bomb that'll blow up," she said, with a smile, "but I know you can handle it."

Not sure about the strange mood he found her in, he walked closer. "Did you need something? Are you okay? I expected you to sleep through the night. I did wonder about stopping in and letting you know I phoned the hospital."

"How is he?" she asked.

"He'll be just fine. He's out of surgery right now."

She smiled. "That is great news. He's a good man."

"I'm pretty sure you've told me that time and time again," he noted, with a smile. "I don't know if he realizes just how much of a cheerleader he has in you."

She shrugged. "I think a lot of people would feel the same. We've been at his side for a lot of cases, watching him pull off miracles, saving the lives of patients who we were pretty sure were done for. So, I know most people would feel the way I do."

"Maybe," he conceded, "but it will still give me nightmares, remembering how you taunted the gunman."

"I didn't taunt him," she clarified in protest. "Well, maybe a couple times. Still, I talked to him. I figured, if a little bit of humanity remained in him, I could convince him to spare all three of us. If not, maybe I could spend a few minutes extending whatever time we had, so if you had a plan"—she gave him an eye roll—"then you would have had time to put it into play."

"Yeah?"

"What I didn't realize was that you *did* have a plan and that you were probably just waiting for me to shut up, so you could implement it."

His lips quirked, as he smiled. "That might have been part of it. Yet *you* did *you*, and it worked out well."

She smiled. "Sometimes things do work out for the best." She got up and walked over to him. "I also decided to make another change."

"What change is that?" he asked warily, as she approached.

She placed a hand on his chest and slowly dropped it downward. "We haven't known each other very long."

"I know," he jumped in. "It's why I suggested we take some time to get to know each other."

"And you're probably right," she agreed. "We should take some time to get to know each other. I'm just not sure that your idea of *time* and mine will be the same."

His eyebrows shot up, as his body started to respond to the presence of a beautiful woman. With Amber, he had tapped down every physical response he possibly could, so he didn't end up in this situation, and yet here she was, playing with fire.

"Are you sure? Are you certain you want to go in this direction?" he asked hesitantly, as her finger slipped along the edge of the towel wrapped around his hips and then slipped inside. She let her finger drift all the way from one hip to the other. He swallowed hard and whispered, "You're playing with fire."

"I am, but I do have a plan. The thing is, … I suspect that, for whatever reason, your history will make you want to drag this out for a long time, to see if going down this path is something you're prepared to do."

His eyebrows drew down, as he contemplated her for a moment. "Is that wrong?"

"No, it's not wrong," she replied, "but not all of us want to wait. Not all of us want to be alone in bed, while you sort it out. I would just as soon you sort it out while we're together, and we can work on problem-solving as we go."

His lips twitched. "That's a good idea to you, is it?" She played with the knot in the towel, as she slowly undid it, staring up at him, her lips twitching, with a twinkle in her eyes, making him fall in love a little bit more with her.

"Yes," she said, "I think it's a great idea. I think you're an incredibly beautiful human being, both inside and out. You're incredibly capable, even though I haven't had a chance to see everything you can do."

"But I thought you wanted to take things slow and easy, so as not to get hurt again." He frowned at her.

She nodded. "I get it. Why would anybody want to get hurt again, but, in your case, I think you'll just have to accept at face value that it won't happen with us."

He narrowed his gaze, as her words slammed into his chest. "We haven't known each other very long," he pointed out hesitantly.

"You keep saying that, but"—she tapped his chest—"don't you think you know me?"

He stared down at her, seeing her expression, the emotions in her eyes. "Maybe," he replied cautiously.

"More than maybe," she clarified. "You are the one who broached the topic of a relationship already."

"Sure, … you know, over time."

"Yeah, well, guess what? You might not get as much time to think about it as you would like." When he shook his head, she nodded. "I won't rush you. If you don't want me in your bed tonight, then that's your choice. It would be the first time I have been rejected, and I can't say that I would like it much, but I certainly won't force you."

She drew her nail down his chest, then over to one nipple, and added, "But I won't be very patient either, so I can give you tonight. I can give you tomorrow. I can give you a week, maybe even a month," she offered, "but no way I can give you more than that."

"And if I don't within that month?"

She laughed. "Then I'll just have to come after you myself."

"And that's not what this is all about?" he asked warily.

"Gosh, no," she said, with a laugh. "This is you having a choice, you getting to say yes or no, and, if you choose no, that's fine." She shrugged. "I'll check in again in another week or something like that." He frowned at her, and she nodded. "See? That's what being patient and giving you time to make the decision is all about. Now me? I would jump into that bed right now because I already know."

"Already know what?" he asked, studying her.

"I already know that I want everything you've got to give and that I want to see just who you are on the inside, on a day-to-day basis. That includes sharing a bed with you, waking up to see your face, holding you in my arms, and being held in yours," she whispered, as she leaned in closer, her warm breath brushing against his. "But I also know what it's like to be hurt, and I know what it's like to not trust, so I'm willing to give you time," she repeated, her lips just a hair's breath away from his.

Mixed emotions filled his heart and soul. He'd never met anyone like her. Not this honest. Not this open. Jasper knew his expressive face exposed all the emotions he felt just now.

"So, how about I go back to my bed, and you can just tell me which way you want to go?"

As she was lifted into the air, she let out a shriek. Then he gently placed her on his bed, before he held her close to him. Looking down at her, he asked, "So, is that enough of a decision for you?"

She burst out laughing. "It's nice to know you can take action at home too, when you need to."

He rolled his eyes at that. "I don't think action will be a problem," he murmured, as he thrust his hips against her, loving the shudders she gave in reaction, "but this is very cheeky of you."

"*Nah*," she replied. "I'm just somebody who knows what she wants and doesn't want to give you too much time to wait."

"What's wrong with waiting?" he murmured, as he nuzzled his nose against her.

"There's waiting, and then there's waiting," she muttered, followed by a chuckle. "There's waiting because you have a religious conviction, a physical reason, or have made a particular decision, or something along that line. And then there's waiting because you're scared of making a wrong decision. Sometimes you just have to jump in with both feet and trust. And I get that trust is hard for you right now, but I have faith that you'll make the right decision," she whispered, as she wiggled her hips beneath him.

He chuckled. "I do like the way you think."

"Good," she murmured, "so, we'll give this a try and see where it goes. We won't worry about who'll get hurt or who won't get hurt because we'll give it our all and see just what we've got, right?"

"And if I say no?" he teased.

"In that case, I might just have to work at convincing you again."

"I'm not against being convinced," he added, followed by joyful laughter. "As a matter of fact, it'll take me a long time to forget your coming into my bedroom tonight."

"Who said you need to forget it? I figured I would keep doing this every night, until you give in."

He burst out laughing and asked, "You mean, I was supposed to hold out longer?"

"*Nah*, I knew you would be a sucker anyway."

"And why is that?" he asked, smiling down at her.

"Because, as you said, something is between us, and … we both want it, and we both want each other. We want what we want, and nobody likes to wait," she explained. "We're adults. We're past that stage of life where we're worried about playing games."

"You think so?"

"It's very much about reaching out and grabbing what life has to offer because you can lose it way too quickly," she stated. "You and I both know what evil bodes for us out there, and we're just the people who want to take every moment and to make the most of it."

HE LOWERED HIS head and gently kissed her, but she wanted more. She wrapped her arms tightly around his neck, thrust her hips up against him and rubbed back and forth. When he lifted his head, he was panting. She nodded. "You don't get to be easy, and you don't get to be soft, and you don't get to be gentle and to think that you'll hurt my leg," she murmured. "I want every damn thing you have to give." She poked him in the chest and then some.

"Do you?" he asked, a glint in his eyes. "What if you can't take all of me?"

"Try me," she dared him, a grin on her face, and she pulled his head down and whispered, "Go ahead. Give it your best shot."

Amber might have done it as a joke, but Jasper took it as a dare. By the time he lifted his head from his deep, passionate, rousing kiss, she was mindless jelly. She gasped. "Oh my God, I've unleashed the devil."

"Oh, I don't know about the devil," he said, as he trailed kisses down the neck of her nightie before pulling it up and off so that she was completely nude beneath him. She realized it was long gone and only felt his heated skin against her sleek, heated skin. With her nightgown now restricting her arms, he held them up high above her head. With one heavy thigh across her good leg, he kept her imprisoned for his ministrations.

His tender kisses, gentle strokes, suckling, tiny little nips and bites, all had her shuddering and crying out for him in joy and pain, combined with need. When he finally slid atop her and sank deep inside, she reacted instantly and then came apart without any warning. He started to move, and she came, again and again, and, by the time he exploded above her, she was already in a place of complete and unrelenting joy.

When he rolled off to the side and pulled her up against him, he whispered, "Are you okay?"

She wrapped her arms around him, then kissed his chest and murmured, "Better than okay."

"Good, that's what happens when you dare me."

She chuckled. "Give me a chance to catch my breath, and we'll go for round two."

His laughter roared through the bedroom. "That's sounds good to me too, but first you need sleep."

"Just me?" she asked, tilting her head back to look up at him.

"No," he murmured, "both of us need sleep." Then he pulled her tightly into his arms and held her close.

Just as she was about to doze off, she asked, "Did you have your meeting?"

"I did," he murmured. "Masters will take the lead on this next leg of Mason's case. He'll track down everything there is to find about the gunman we faced. It appears he may have been acquainted with somebody both he and the sniper knew in common."

She looked up at him and smiled. "And will you stay here with me?"

He gave her a breathtaking smile and murmured, "Sounds like an absolutely wonderful punishment." And, with that, he kissed her and whispered, "Now go to sleep."

This concludes Book 1 of Man Down: Jasper.

Read about Masters: Man Down, Book 2

Man Down:
Masters
(Book #2)

There is no greater motive than bloodlust, DNA, and revenge mixed up in a cocktail of hatred ...

Masters has joined Jasper's investigation team, when they realize another investigator went missing four months ago, yet his case is on hold. Part of the issue is that Masters needs to figure out who on the existing team is trustworthy. He reaches out to the missing investigator's sister, looking for answers.

Elizabeth has been seeking answers over her brother's disappearance ever since the last time she spoke to him. With no leads, no tips, and no sign of him, the case ran cold. To her, it seemed no one cared. Having Masters show up at her door, asking questions all over again, sparks anger and hope in her.

Maybe this time they can find out what happened to the

only family Elizabeth has left …

Find Book 2 here!

To find out more visit Dale Mayer's website.

https://geni.us/DMSMDMasters

MASTERS WOODROW ENTERED the building where the investigators worked, which was dark. Turning on the lights, he headed to the small area that Jasper had used as an office. Sitting down and using his log-in credentials, Masters started the research he needed to do. When he heard a noise, he looked up to see Sam glaring at him. Masters stared back at him. "You got a problem? You take it up with Jasper." Then he returned to his research.

"It's Jasper I've got a problem with," he barked.

Masters shrugged, refusing to face Sam. "Then take it up with the brass. Not my problem."

"Seriously, you're on this team now too?"

"I am," he declared.

"What about Jasper?"

"Jasper is too. He's getting some much-needed rest right now. In case you didn't hear about the mess happening today, he's been busy."

Sam shrugged. "It wasn't all that bad."

"If that's what you think, you don't have all the details." Masters stopped, looked up at him, and intensely studied the man for the first time. Sam looked to be about late forties, a hothead by the sound of it, and a little bit gone to pot. He had a good-sized middle rim of flab all the way around his belly, just above his belt loops. His coloring was pale, a little bit blotchy, and his hair was thinning on top already.

"What's your problem with Jasper anyway?"

"He walked in here like he was the boss and took over. He already knew Morgan's the boss."

"Morgan was an *acting* boss," Masters clarified, narrowing his gaze at Sam. "How come you didn't tell your bosses how you felt?"

Sam shifted uneasily and scoffed. "You're just like him, aren't you? You're probably friends. Is that how you got the job?"

"I don't have to do things like that," he replied. "My reputation precedes me, as does Jasper's, as does Mason's. This is what I do. I was coming in to take a job on this base as it was, yet in a slightly different position. However, after seeing Mason shot down right in front of me, you can bet I wanted in on it."

"Oh, yeah, shot in front of you, but you didn't do anything to stop it, did you?"

"It would be a little hard to stop a sniper plan set up days, if not months in advance," he stated. He noted Sam stood unsteadily in front of him. "Are you drunk?"

"No, I'm not drunk," he snapped. "What are you doing here at this hour of the night?"

"What are *you* doing here at this hour of the night, drunk or not?" Not liking anything about him, Masters added, "Either you need to get the hell out of here or sit down and do some work. I am working myself. So you choose what you're doing, but make a decision now."

"And if I don't?" Sam asked, his hands in his pockets, but, sure enough, he remained unsteady on his feet.

Masters got up, walked closer, and smelled the alcohol. "You get your drunk ass out of here," he ordered. "Leave your key card behind, and do not come in until you contact me and I've met you outside of work somewhere long enough to confirm that you're sober."

"What are you gonna—"

"And, if I find out that you're not sober and that you can't stay sober for forty-eight hours straight, you'll be under drug testing and suspended from work," Masters declared calmly, as he turned Sam around and gave him a shove toward the exit door.

Protesting the whole way, Sam started to slur his words to the point that Masters was worried he would have to pick him up to toss him out.

When he got him outside the building, a couple other guys were hanging around, loudly laughing and talking and drinking. "Are you with them?"

"So what if I am?"

"That's fine, but, in the meantime, you are not allowed to drive tonight either."

"You can't stop me," Sam bellowed.

But Masters braced him, quickly shoving him against the wall, taking his car keys and his office key card. "Now get yourself home."

"How the hell am I supposed to do that? You just took my wheels."

"I did, and I'll take even more, the longer you stand here. Now get lost," he snapped. Then he watched as Sam stumbled away.

Shaking his head, Masters returned to the office and quickly sent Jasper a text. Masters wasn't sure what the hell was going on, but how the hell did that guy Sam keep his job here? Maybe they did need a couple new people on this investigation team. He sent a quick text to Morgan, asking him about Sam's condition as well.

When the phone rang, Morgan was on the other end.

"What the hell are you doing there?"

"I'm here because Jasper is at home after an incident tonight," he explained. "I'm working on Mason's case. Found Sam in the office, stumbling drunk."

Silence came on the other end. "Oh, damn."

"Meaning?"

"Meaning, he fell off the stupid wagon again."

"And how much of a problem is that?"

"It shouldn't be a problem at all."

"I just took his car keys off him and his access card." He picked up the card and frowned. "Except for one thing."

"What's that?" Morgan asked.

"The card key that I took off Sam doesn't have his name on it."

"What do you mean?"

"The key I have in my hand, which I just took off Sam, has a different name on it. … Nicholas."

"Nicholas, Nicholas Woodrow?" Morgan asked.

Masters frowned at the last name. He had no relative that he knew of by the name of Nicholas. Yet easier to remember the guy's name, for sure. Masters twisted the key card in the light to see it better, noting the tone change in Morgan's reply. "Yes, Nicholas Woodrow. Why? You know him?"

"Yeah, he disappeared from our department and the base about four months ago," he shared. "He was involved in another case on Coronado base."

"What do you mean, *another case*?"

"Nicholas was working on another shooting."

Find Book 2 here!

To find out more visit Dale Mayer's website.

https://geni.us/DMSMDMasters

Author's Note

Thank you for reading Jasper: Man Down, Book 1! If you enjoyed the book, please take a moment and leave a short review.

Dear reader,

I love to hear from readers, and you can contact me at my website: www.dalemayer.com or at my Facebook author page. To be informed of new releases and special offers, sign up for my newsletter or follow me on BookBub. And if you are interested in joining Dale Mayer's Reader Group, here is the Facebook sign up page.
http://geni.us/DaleMayerFBGroup

Cheers,
Dale Mayer

About the Author

Dale Mayer is a *USA Today* best-selling author, best known for her SEALs military romances, her Psychic Visions series, and her Lovely Lethal Garden cozy series. Her contemporary romances are raw and full of passion and emotion (Broken But … Mending, Hathaway House series). Her thrillers will keep you guessing (Kate Morgan, By Death series), and her romantic comedies will keep you giggling (*It's a Dog's Life*, a stand-alone novella; and the Broken Protocols series, starring Charming Marvin, the cat).

Dale honors the stories that come to her—and some of them are crazy, break all the rules and cross multiple genres!

To go with her fiction, she also writes nonfiction in many different fields, with books available on résumé writing, companion gardening, and the US mortgage system. All her books are available in print and ebook format.

Connect with Dale Mayer Online

Dale's Website – www.dalemayer.com

Twitter – @DaleMayer

Facebook Page – geni.us/DaleMayerFBFanPage

Facebook Group – geni.us/DaleMayerFBGroup

BookBub – geni.us/DaleMayerBookbub

Instagram – geni.us/DaleMayerInstagram

Goodreads – geni.us/DaleMayerGoodreads

Newsletter – geni.us/DaleNews